Waste not your Tears

Waste not your Tears

Vivienne Ndlovu

WEAVER
W
PRESS

First published by
Baobab Books, Harare, 1994

This second edition published by
Weaver Press, Box A1922, Avondale, Harare
<www.weaverpresszimbabwe.com>

This revised edition, 2018

Typeset by Weaver Press
Cover Design: Farai Wallace, Harare.

ISBN: 978-1-77922-331-9 (p/b)
ISBN: 978-1-77922-326-6 (e-pub)w

Vivienne Ndlovu is an Irish Zimbabwean writer who works for SAFAIDS in Harare. Her fiction includes *For want of a Totem*, and the short stories 'Homecoming' in *Writing Still* (2003), 'Kurima' in *Writing Now* (2005), and 'Bare Bones' in *Women Writing Zimbabwe* (2008).

Foreword

Waste Not your Tears was written and first published in 1994 when the HIV epidemic in Zimbabwe was not yet at its peak and effective treatment was not yet available. It is also based on the true story of a young woman and her partner who were early victims of the virus, but brave enough to tell their stories. The novel is a powerful reminder of the early days of the AIDS pandemic and the dreadful consequences of untreated HIV infection. I encourage everyone to read it and appreciate the tremendous strides made in HIV prevention and treatment over the last two decades.

At one point up to 3,000 people a week were dying of AIDS-related illnesses. This may be hard to believe today, when effective and affordable antiretroviral therapy (ART) and prevention of mother-to-child transmission (PMTCT) services are readily available. HIV is now a long-term medical condition, manageable with medication, much like high blood pressure (BP) or diabetes.

There is one important difference. HIV is primarily contracted through unprotected sexual intercourse (sex without a condom) and today, the highest numbers of new infections are in young people between the ages of 15 and 24; new infections in girls and young women are also higher than in boys and men. Although treatment is now available, prevention is always the best option.

It is important that young people appreciate the importance of looking after their sexual health by delaying first sex and failing that, by making sure they use male or female condoms every time. Limiting the number of sexual partners and avoiding much older sexual partners are important ways of maintaining your sexual and reproductive health and preventing the transmission of the HIV infection. Lack of money often leads young people to have transactional sex (sex for payment of fees, for food, cell phones, clothes...) but it is hard to insist on condom use in these circumstances, increasing the risk of HIV infection and unintended pregnancy.

Unintended pregnancy in young girls is a major cause of reproductive illness and maternal death; condoms protect against HIV and other sexually transmitted infections, as well as unintended pregnancy.

With HIV infection, the earlier a person begins treatment – before the virus has caused serious damage to their immune system – the better for their long-term health.

There is a group of young people in Zimbabwe who may be unaware of their HIV infection. These are young people born before PMTCT was widely available. Even today, some mothers fail to complete the full course of PMTCT, resulting in them passing HIV on to their babies. For this reason, EVERYONE should know their HIV status.

Get tested for HIV today. If you are negative, then you can take steps to make sure you stay negative; and if you are HIV positive, you can seek treatment, maintain your health and look forward to a long and healthy life.

Lois Chingandu
Executive Director SAFAIDS
April 2018

Chapter One

The girl beside him stirred in her sleep, and made small moaning sounds, as though she were having troubled dreams. 'So you might girl, so you might.' He thought wryly to himself. He looked around the room in which they had spent the night. She had been indifferent in bed like so many of these whores, and he thought with regret of the soft compliant body of Loveness.

Loveness. There was no doubt about her love for him. He knew with absolute certainty that she had never, and now, would never love any man other than him. But she had left him, and at the thought the anger crept through his body like small licking flames creeping from his gut till they finally reached and settled in his loins. He jabbed his elbow into the girl's ribs, not gently, and she woke up with a cry of pain and surprise, her still sleepy eyes looked into his, and he immediately moved on top of her, ignoring her protests. He was unnecessarily rough but what did it matter. She was only a whore anyway, and he had to still the fire that seemed to rage through him unquenched. Not that Loveness had stilled it. He had been unmoved by her slavish love for him, even irritated by her, but he could not reconcile himself to the fact that she had left him.

Now he was alone, and he knew that his time was running out. He could feel the disease gathering momentum within him. Soon he would need someone to feed him and care for him, and he could not rely on his family. His mother had expected that he, her only son, would provide for her in her old age, but here he was thirty-seven and dying. Of no more use to her than her daughters.

Sated, despite the disinterested body beneath him, he looked down at her. The girl had turned her head towards the door and her face showed only bored resignation as he rolled over and away from her. The previous night he had been drinking in the Queen's Garden, and the girl had joined him at his table. For once he had not been looking for a woman, had been content just to drink himself into a state of stupor while he wallowed in self-pity over Loveness' desertion. But this stupid whore had settled herself beside him and had even been willing to pay for some of his beers.

The prostitute, disappointed as so many times before, stared at the wall and watched, as though in a film, the events that had brought her here to this room, this bed, this man.

'Aren't you going to marry me?' she asked her beloved once more in her schoolgirl innocence when she realised she was pregnant.

'Marry you?' he had scoffed. 'I haven't finished my education. I've been accepted at the university. I can't have a wife and child holding me back!' and he had disappeared into the big city, untraceable among the throngs of clever university students to whom she did not even dare speak, leaving her to deal with her outraged parents. Later, she had left the child with them – at least they had stood by her – and she had come to Harare to look for work. But she had no education, and the only job she could find was as a domestic worker.

In that she was lucky. Her first employer was a young couple, with one small child who, despite her fair skin and blue eyes, took the place of the daughter she had left behind. But then they had decided to leave Zimbabwe and go down South, and she had bidden them a tearful goodbye. Before they left, they hurriedly put an advert in The Tribune and the first person who answered it and came to see her looked her up and down as if he were buying a horse, asked the mistress if she could work, and said, 'She'll do.'

After she had been working for him for a few months, she went to make his bed one morning and found him still in it. As she retreated and closed the door again, he called her to come into the room and asked her to fluff up his pillows. As she did so, his hand crept under her skirt. She pulled away from his whispering, 'No, baas, no,' but he persisted, and holding her still said, 'no problem girl. I'll give you a bit extra in your pay. You're a pretty little thing you know.' And because she didn't want to lose her job, and didn't know what else she could do, she did not resist, and many nights he would call her to the house when her work was done, and send her back to her quarters when the moon was high. It went on like that for a long time. She even grew quite fond of him for he treated her gently. Then one evening he told her to prepare a special meal and when the doorbell rang, a white woman stood there. That night he didn't call her, and when she went to the house next day she found the woman making coffee.

A few weeks later, the baas called her in and said, 'Wish me makorokoto girl!' He never called by her name. 'Wish me makorokoto. She's going to marry me. That madam you saw,' and he danced with her around the kitchen. She smiled at him, and then he said, 'Of course it's the end of the line for you and me girl. Can't have you being around and sharing secrets with the baas now can we?' he leered at her, and took her hand, leading her to the bedroom. 'Just one last time, eh? To celebrate.' When he was done he gave her her pay and twenty dollars extra, and told her to go that same day.

'But please baas. Please can't you help me to find another job, baas!'

'I've no time to waste on that, girl. You'll be alright. You're a pretty little thing.' He kissed his hand, blowing the kiss at her as he left for work. But she didn't find another job, and within a few weeks she realised that she had been caught again. The baas had practised withdrawal, and it had always worked. Only when she missed her period did she remember that that last time; she remembered the wetness. So now she had two children to feed, one a pale coloured child who looked quite like the baas. She thought of going to him for help, but she heard he had got married and he wouldn't want her turning up on the doorstep to show his new bride their son. Eventually she returned to Harare, but still she failed to find a job.

Then came the evening she was taken to a bar by a cousin of the family she was staying with. He bought her a beer, and for the first time she understood why men liked to drink. It gave her a pleasant floating sensation, and she was filled with confidence. The cousin laughed when she told him she liked it and bought her another. Later, couples began to dance, and the cousin led her to the dance floor. She danced and enjoyed herself as she hadn't done since she had left school, and when a well-dressed young man offered to buy her a drink she accepted. When the music ended she and the young man were still together but she could see no sign of the cousin. The young man asked her where she stayed. 'Kambuzuma,' she said.

'Don't you have anywhere closer?'

'What do you mean?' she asked, by now quite drunk.

'You know, somewhere we can go together. We have to

get to know each other better,' he said meaningfully. The girl realised that this man had been buying her drinks all night – perhaps he would get nasty if she didn't go along with him and so when he suggested a room in a cheap hotel she agreed. Next morning he left her with twenty dollars. She didn't even ask him for it. He just left it on the cheap dresser as he went out the door. The twenty dollars was almost like a gift from heaven. So easy – she thought. As a domestic worker she would have to work a week to earn that sort of money, and without a reference she had little hope of finding another job. She had to earn money somehow and so she said to herself, 'Maybe this way, for a while, until I get myself on my feet. At least I can send my children some money.'

That had been six years ago. No more children. She had learned about the pill, but she never did seem to get back on her feet and so here she was, in the Queen's Garden, looking for company tonight, for a sympathetic face. For someone to listen to her story. She was tired of the way of life forced on her by prostitution. She wanted nothing more than to find a man and settle with him to bring up her children. But she no longer believed there were men you could live with, whom you could trust, and still her whole being cried out for the impossible. As a child, she had never imagined any future ahead of her except as some man's wife, the mother of his children and she had loved her first child's father with all her heart. He had denied her. They had all denied her, yet still she believed what she had been brought up to believe – a woman's place was to look after a man, that without a man she was nothing.

Roderick hadn't expected the sex worker to sleep with him, not without a condom at least, for even to himself now, he looked emaciated, suspect. But it seemed that even the prostitutes didn't believe in the reality of AIDS, and he laughed to himself as he debated whether to tell her she had been well paid for last night's work.

'What's the matter?' the girl asked him. 'Why are you laughing?'

'Oh, nothing that would interest you, mukadzi,' he replied, pulling on his clothes, and throwing a ten dollar note at her.

Ten minutes later he was on his way to the offices of the AIDS Welfare Centre, whistling to himself, as he thought of the sympathy he would get when he told them about Loveness. Yet while he thought of what he would tell them this time, a small lingering trouble danced under the surface of his thoughts. Being alone. It was the only thing that truly bothered him and without Loveness, he was alone, however many people he might be with. He didn't want to be alone so that was what he would tell those white liberals at the Centre. He would weep and tell them he was afraid, and he was lonely. Loveness had deserted him, and he couldn't be alone. Maybe they would find somewhere else he could stay. Doctor Baker was beginning to get on his nerves. The other day when they were talking the doctor had asked about Loveness and Roderick got the distinct feeling that maybe someone had told him that she wasn't an HIV girl when he had brought her to live with him. Although he couldn't allow the thought to surface, it lurked at the back of his mind. What would happen to him if they found out that he was the one who infected Loveness, that he knew she was a virgin when they got together?

Then his usual arrogance surfaced again and he thought, 'She was a real stupid one.' She could have exposed him to everyone, especially that time when she was pregnant with the baby and he had gone to Harare looking for a bit of fun. He was bored with her by then, and wanted to get rid of her, but everyone knew they were living together. That had been a mistake, letting her move in, but he had needed someone to cook for him, to feel beside him when he woke up afraid in the long dark nights. And Loveness had always covered for him, even after the baby died. But that had killed the last spark in her, just as it had in him: it finally made him understand that he too might really die. But he was Roderick. Invincible. Lady-killer.

In his short life he had six 'wives' including Loveness, although he hadn't married any of them, never paid lobola and he had left all of them weeping for him, begging for him to stay. He laughed to himself as he walked down the street. Lady-killer. That was him. Only now it was for real.

Chapter Two

He hadn't understood what it was all about at first. The blood transfusion service had come round to the factory where he worked as they did every six months or so, and he joined the queue to give blood. He had started to donate because one of the nurses had been a real looker and he'd figured it was a good way to get talking to her. It had worked too, and she'd ended up in his bed like so many others. Once he was on their list, the blood transfusion people looked for him every time they came and he'd always obliged. Then later, he got a letter from them telling him that he should go to the doctor for tests. He didn't think much about it, but he went along to the company doctor and when the results came out, and the doctor talked to him, nothing he said made any sense. 'Maybe it's *runyoka*,' he thought. 'That woman's husband is a sly old fool. Maybe he went to a *n'anga* to fix me.'

But he didn't get sick, and he would have forgotten all about it except that a few weeks later he was called in by the personnel officer and told that they didn't need him any more. He had only been with the company for a while, and had had a few days off with a bad hangover so he wasn't surprised. But then, after he collected his pay cheque, the nurse from the clinic called him in and asked him to go and see the people at the AIDS Welfare Centre. He had never heard of them before. He dimly recalled reading something about a disease called AIDS but he didn't know much about it. Anyway, the place was a welfare centre which meant there must be money around somewhere so he decided to pay them a visit.

The people there were very serious – the sort of sincere, concerned kind that he despised. He listened to what they had to say, but he didn't really believe it. It sounded too much like one of those stories of religious damnation out of the Bible. They kept lecturing him about sex, and telling him he should make his peace with God because he was going to die. But he felt fine and he reckoned the whole thing was just a plot to spoil one of life's few pleasures.

The AWC people asked him where he lived, and he told them he had been evicted because he had lost his job, though in fact his landlord, fed up with his tenant's drunken ways, had finally told him to leave. It was just a useful coincidence, but the AWC people were very worried about it, more so than Roderick himself, and they had introduced him to Doctor Baker. Doctor Baker was involved in the AIDS education campaign, and after talking to Roderick for a short while, he decided that maybe he could make use of him by taking him along to schools to speak to the children about AIDS. It would have more impact if there was someone actually there in front of them who had HIV.

'Roderick's English is good, and he's articulate. The only problem is I'm not sure he appreciates what's going on, and what his being HIV positive really means,' he said to Peter. Peter had had the task of sitting down and talking with the new arrival about the centre, and about HIV and AIDS.

'Maybe I'll have a chat with him about it before he leaves. How does he seem to you?'

'I agree that he doesn't really seem to have taken it in,' replied Peter, 'but we'll keep him here for a while, talk to him some more. He doesn't seem anxious to go anywhere.'

'Maybe he doesn't have anywhere else to go,' said Doctor Baker thoughtfully.

Meanwhile, Roderick sitting in the waiting room, was surrounded by posters saying things like: 'Your next sexual partner could be that very special person, the one who gives you AIDS', the words surrounded by a huge Valentine's heart. On the table were leaflets about health and AIDS, and to pass the time he had read some of them, growing more and more uneasy as the information began to filter through to his consciousness. Could all this be true? He read an article about the origins of the disease, and discovered that there were those who believe that it had been developed by the Americans as part of their biological warfare programme, which had somehow gone out of control. More than any other theory he read in that office that day, this one struck him as plausible; made him consider that for once his invincible self might actually have been breached.

He had a natural antipathy towards America and Americans and hated the sight of those fat, wealthy American tourists. Slowly he absorbed what was going on, what had happened to him over the last few days, and he realised that however much he despised the AWC people, he actually believed what they were telling him. He believed that he might be dying.

It was in this state of newly found sobriety and fear that Doctor Baker returned to talk to him. He looked at the tall handsome young man, now sitting alertly on a chair in the corner and was filled with pity at the circumstances which had brought them together. In their first brief chat he had been impressed by his eloquence. It wasn't often that he came across an African like Roderick. He was more used to the submissive sort who worked as gardeners or domestics. Independence had certainly changed things, he thought to himself, as he opened the glass-topped door and called Roderick into his office.

By now, Roderick was extremely anxious although he did his best to hide it. He kept saying to himself over and over again, 'I'm going to die, I'm going to die,' but somewhere along the way, as the doctor talked gently to him and he heard the sympathy in his voice, denial took over again. He looked at his hands, at his arms, just as later he looked at his erect manhood, and he saw nothing. Nothing to mark out as different from anyone else, no mark of the beast that identified *him*, Roderick, as doomed, and he thought with false bravado, 'Everyone's dying. Life is a terminal disease.' Then he was listening again to what the old man was saying, and he suddenly understood that he might be onto a good thing.

'Of course, if you agree to help, we'll pay you. After all, you would be doing it in working hours. I'm sure you realise just how important it is that we get this message through to the youth in the schools... And I understand it was because of this blood test that you lost your job. You may have difficulty in finding another. If you help us out, it will tide you over for a while. Will you do it?' He looked kindly at the young man who, he believed, was still in a state of shock.

Roderick was thinking very fast. This was a soft touch. Maybe he'd chanced upon a way of freeloading – no more work! Of course, he'd have to play the good African 'boy', but that was easy.

'I know it's not easy to think about standing up and saying you've got this disease Roderick, but it's the only way to educate people about it, to make them accept that it's real, even when there are no outward signs.'

Roderick sat back in his chair, and speaking in his most earnest voice, said, 'Doctor, I agree with everything you say. I've got nothing more to lose now have I? I've lost my job, my home...'

'You've lost your home too?'

'Well, yes. You see, I was a bit behind with my rent anyway. I had to send my ex-wife the money for school fees for my daughter and when the landlord heard I'd been given the sack, he gave me a week's notice. That's my next job. To find somewhere else to live.'

As he said all this, Roderick hung his head, and sounded as dejected and hopeless as possible. It was half true, like so much of what Roderick said. Bits of truth littered his life like rubbish on the Harare streets. Of course, he would never send school fees for a girl child. In fact, he had no contact at all with any of the women he had lived with.

'This is a disgrace,' the doctor was saying. He continued enthusiastically, 'You see why we must fight this thing, Roderick? We must go public over this insidious evil in our midst. We must expose it to the cold light of day, until people see that there, but for the grace of God, go all of us! How can they throw a dying man out on the streets like that!'

Roderick looked up at the old man hopefully.

Doctor Baker had been one of the first people in the country to recognise the dangers of AIDS. In front of him he saw yet another victim of the lifestyle forced upon the local people by the whites and their tribal trust lands, where the women stayed alone bringing up the children while the men worked in the towns. Now he was incensed at the idea that the country's future might be destroyed by this evil disease, and as he looked at the personable young man in front of him he remembered that the servant's quarters at his home was a double one, and that one room was empty. He could have the electricity fixed up; Roderick could move in there. Old Noah, his domestic worker-cum-gardener would probably be happy to have some company, and he would certainly appreciate having electricity.

Before he had thought about it any further he heard himself saying, 'Roderick, I think I may be able to help you. I have an empty room in my servant's quarters. I'm in the process of getting them fixed up, electricity, a shower and so on. Would you be interested in moving in there? You'd be near at hand if we needed to get in touch about you giving a talk somewhere. We can make sure it's out of Harare if you like, then you'll be less likely to bump into someone you know.' Then he remembered that Roderick hadn't yet agreed with his proposal about helping them. He knew it was a big step to take.

Roderick could hardly believe his luck! What a chance. Mind you, it was probably a disgusting little room, but beggars can't be choosers. This was an opportunity he wasn't going to miss. Who knew what else he might be able to get out of the old fellow?

'Well sir,' he said hesitantly, 'that's really kind of you. But how much rent do you think you might be asking? As you know my situation is a bit uncertain…'

'Why Roderick, I hadn't thought of charging you anything. At least not until the place is fixed up. I'm sure we can come to some agreement. If you do some talks for us, we'll work out some mutually agreeable sum.'

'That's good of you, doctor. I don't know what to say. But of course I'll help you out. If it's the only way to beat this thing then it's worth a try.'

'That's grand, Roderick. Just grand. Why don't you come

back here about five o'clock, and I'll show the place to you. Don't expect anything special now. It's a bit of a mess at the moment but we'll fix it up. It'll give you something to occupy yourself with,' and he ushered Roderick out of the office.

Both men were filled with a warm glow; Doctor Baker because he felt he'd been able to kill two birds with one stone – to help this sensitive young man who was coping so well with such devastating news, and because he'd at last found someone who had the courage to stand up and tell people, 'I'm infected with HIV. I'm going to die.' On Roderick's part he reckoned he was onto the best thing that had ever happened to him. He had already dismissed the idea that he might really be dying, and later, his last night in his old lodgings, he had taken a woman home with him and been reassured by the normality of his response to the presence of a female body.

His virility and masculinity had always been important to Roderick. He was the only son in a family of seven girls. His father had almost given up hope of having a son when Roderick came along, and he had grown up spoiled by both parents, and all seven sisters. He had never had to do anything much himself, but he was very bright and had enjoyed school. Then one evening his father was killed in a fight on the way home from a beer drink, and Roderick's bright future had been cut short. He had intended to go on to do his O-Levels, but with his father dead there was no money for such luxuries as education, even for a boy.

While his mother and sisters were trying to earn enough money to keep themselves alive and to provide the funds for Roderick's school fees, Roderick was entertaining himself as best he could. He spent his days wandering among the villages in the area, and eventually came across a girl about his own age. The girl had been orphaned a few years earlier and since none of her parents' relatives would care for her, she had no alternative but to survive by prostituting herself with the few men who stayed in the village. She was delighted to meet a boy of her own age for a change and to spend time with him and when Roderick finally began to notice her as more than just a playmate, she was equally happy to teach him the joys of sex.

Despite the self-centredness which should have been obvious to anyone who cared to see, Roderick was attractive and charming and women fell for him easily. He lived with a succession of different girls promising each the earth until he grew tired of them and moved on to the next. He never stayed with one for more than a couple of years, but if he had not tired of them sooner, then the birth of a girl child was enough to make him move on. More than anything else he wanted a son. He wanted his son to have the opportunities that had been snatched from him with his father's death.

Although he was shocked by the apparent inevitability of what had happened to him when he first learned about HIV and AIDS, Roderick was always conscious of situations that could be manipulated to his favour, and most of all he was lazy. He moved into Doctor Baker's *khaya*, and kept himself to himself while he was there. It amused him to think of the double life he was leading and how at last he could live without having to work in a dirty, noisy factory, sweating, and earning a pittance. In a surprisingly short time he had adjusted to his new situation and convinced himself that while the disease was real, it wouldn't affect him. For the first few weeks he spent much of his time in the Centre's offices, reading about the disease he was told he had, so that he could talk knowledgeably about it to school children. He developed a controlled schizophrenia that allowed him to behave normally when he was with his family and friends and like a reformed sinner when the need arose. He had never been one for close relationships with other men. Having grown up primarily in the company of his sisters he was more at ease with women, although he was popular and had many acquaintances of the kind who like to compete in their drinking and womanizing.

After he had lived with Doctor Baker for a few months, the doctor asked him if he would mind expanding his activities by spending some time at the Centre, and talking to others who came for advice maybe even, the doctor added, he would consider joining their new venture by talking to factory workers. Roderick was less enthusiastic about this than he had been about visiting schools – talking to children was one thing, but talking to people like himself... Harare wasn't such a big place, sooner or later he was bound to come across someone he knew. But he was comfortable living in the quarters, and he didn't want to rock the boat. He agreed, and for a few weeks things went smoothly.

Then one Sunday morning, he opened a newspaper and saw a photograph of a man who had come out in the open about being HIV positive. He was the first person ever to admit in public that he carried the disease. Roderick studied the article carefully, and listened even more carefully to all the comments made about him, but there was still a strong element of disbelief. People could not accept the idea that someone could carry a disease like this and not get sick for such a long time. They were sure it must be some kind of *muti*. Some people even said they were sure the man must have been paid to say he had the disease, and this set Roderick thinking. Surely there must be more he could squeeze out of this thing. He must speak some more to Doctor Baker.

Consequently, a few weeks later, Roderick found himself a member of a group set up to help HIV positive people support themselves. Then one day, as they were leaving the office after one of their meetings, a photographer appeared from nowhere and took their picture. Another man who had just joined the group, pulled Roderick aside in the confusion and asked if they could go for a drink together. Still blinded by the camera's flash, Roderick agreed.

As they sat drinking their beer, the other man said, 'I have a confession to make Rod.' Roderick looked at him, irritated by the man's familiar attitude, and the man went on, 'You see, I'm not really HIV positive. I'm a reporter. We want to do a story on your group. Bring the whole thing out in the open, have pictures, talk about the work you're doing, and give the whole thing some life. Too many people out there are saying AIDS doesn't exist, or that it's just *runyoka*. What do you think?'

Roderick was angry. Who did this guy think he was, pretending like that, sneaking into the group? But if they had known he was a reporter they would never have let him in...

'I'll have to talk to the AWC about it,' he said, 'see if they think it's a good idea. I'll get back to you.' He pushed his chair aside and drained his beer.

'You can get me at *The Tribune*,' the reporter replied eagerly, 'Nathan Mutamba's the name.'

Roderick left the bar. He went straight to Doctor Baker's house, and knocked loudly on the door. He explained what had happened, much to Doctor Baker's dismay.

'Well Roderick, I'm sorry, but I suppose it was bound to happen sooner or later. What do you want us to do? You know they can't publish your picture under something like this unless you agree to it, so you need have no worries on that score.'

However, Roderick had already seen some possible advantages in having his picture appear in the paper, and couldn't understand why the doctor was so worried. After all, he'd already 'come out' about his disease. What difference could it make if his picture appeared in the paper? He might even get more money.

'I think it's important we come out in the open, Doctor Baker. The AWC could do with some free publicity after all, and it can't make much difference to me now,' he replied.

'But Roderick, are you sure? You realise the stigma that's attached to this, and once you've been in the paper there'll be no hiding it any more.'

'it's okay, Doctor. They can publish the picture, after checking with the other guys, of course, and I'll talk to them.' Yet again the doctor was surprised by Roderick's willingness to co-operate.

In fact, Roderick didn't have any idea what it would mean to appear in the paper in connection with this devil's disease. His limited public exposure had lured him into a false sense of security about it, especially since he had seen the story in the paper about the other guy. As in so many other things, he felt immune to danger or harm. He never imagined that fanatics would write to him, that people would cross the street when they saw him coming. Or that some of his friends would be afraid to be seen with him, afraid that he would infect them just by talking to them, or sharing a cigarette. Although he had told his mother some vague story about where he was living and what he was doing, he hadn't really explained it to her. He had certainly made no attempt to educate his family and friends about the dangers they now faced unknowingly. But then, even if he had understood how people would react, he would probably still have been more attracted by the idea of the publicity, of appearing in the paper, and by the possibility of getting more money.

Roderick and Doctor Baker had gone to the paper's offices where Nathan Mutamba had interviewed him about his sorry story. How he had been infected by his unfaithful wife and had lost his job when his employer found out. He had even lost his home because his landlord was afraid. The next day, the photograph appeared in the paper with only Roderick's face clearly visible. Some of the others had asked that their faces be blanked out, and others were in shadow but Roderick's face was clear for all to see.

The first week was a nightmare. Many of his usual companions refused to have anything more to do with him, and even his family were afraid to share food with him. It was one thing to go and visit schools and factories, talk to people he would never see again and quite another to have effectively told everyone who had ever met him. And he was also finding it more and more difficult to deny the truth of the disease to himself, in the face of his ever-increasing knowledge about it.

Three days after his picture appeared in the paper, Roderick awoke feeling feverish. All his joints ached and his head felt as though it was splitting. He immediately imagined the worst. This was it. He was dying. Although he would have been better off in bed, he made his way to his oldest sister's house. She gave him a reluctant welcome at the door, but seeing that he was ill and afraid, she had to take him in.

He begged her to call Doctor Baker, for in his panic he saw how he had taken his family for granted by not talking to them about his condition before he went public. Lying in bed, he understood how much he needed them and that he had failed to appreciate that they too would be afraid. Doctor Baker would be able to explain things to them properly.

When Doctor Baker had left, Roderick and his two sisters living in Harare, sat and talked. Roderick explained what

Doctor Baker was doing, and how he had given him a place to stay. His sisters were pragmatic. Roderick was not the first in his family to be interested primarily in himself, and when he explained that there were quite a few side benefits in what was going on they were much more relaxed about the situation.

'You see,' he told them, 'I could just as easily be knocked down and killed by an emergency taxi.' This was one of his own ploys for keeping his terror at bay and he was relieved when they laughed their agreement.

As for his mother, as she grew older she had become more and more resigned to the vagaries of her children's behaviour. She had watched her eldest daughter grow bitter and twisted when her husband left her for another woman, and later took her children from her when they were old enough to be of some use to him. And Roderick, her beloved son, treated women as though they were toys made for his pleasure. She no longer attempted to give her children any direction. Now, when she discovered and understood what had happened to Roderick, it was just another example of how little control she had over her life. Everything was turned around. Her only son, whom she had expected would remain to look after her in old age, might now, it seemed, die before her. She had already resigned herself to waiting for death, now it seemed it could be hers, or her son's. Her only certainty was that death would claim them.

To Roderick's surprise and great relief, he recovered quickly from his flu, and his fear quickly forgotten, he used this small triumph to reinforce his conviction that it was all a mistake. Doctor Baker had offered him a repeat blood test, but he wasn't willing to do that. Having a second positive test would frighten him even more and he had no real reason to doubt the truth of the first. He was more than familiar now with the routes of transmission, and his lifestyle and sexual behaviour put him in the high risk category. No. Better to live with the possibility that he might be negative than to be damned with the truth that he was, once and for always, HIV positive.

In the weeks that followed his public announcement, Roderick had many occasions to regret his decision. Why had he been so stupid? For once he even allowed himself to think that his vanity was his downfall. He hadn't been able to resist the idea of having his picture in the paper, whatever the reason. He hadn't understood the difference between being known and being notorious. By the end of the third week after his picture had appeared, he had begun to believe that there were only costs and no benefits, when he was approached by an organisation that wanted him to help them in their AIDS awareness campaign. If he agreed to work with them they would give him a small regular monthly income, 'for life' as they put it. As he signed the contract, Roderick congratulated himself that he had made the right decision after all. In another two weeks his revelation would be forgotten and though he had lost some of his mates, on balance he felt he had gained a great deal more.

Chapter Three

A girl like Loveness didn't have a chance, not with someone like Roderick. She was young and naïve, and had no real experience of men except for her father; no mother to set an example or to teach her about life. Her mother had died giving birth to her and her twin brother and though her father did his best he couldn't look after two small babies alone so on his sister's advice, he had arranged for them to stay in an orphanage. Mr Mukafa had loved his wife dearly and although he couldn't look after the babies on his own he had no intention of forgetting about them, or of letting them forget that although they stayed in an orphanage they still had a father who loved them.

At every opportunity he would go to the orphanage to see his babies and to talk to Mrs Banda, the matron, whose responsibility they were. He was an affectionate man and the children grew up always aware of the difference between themselves and the other children. They knew they had a father who loved them and another place to call home. About their mother they were less sure. Mr Mukafa never spoke about their mother – he found it too painful. As very young children they considered their family to be all the other children in the orphanage and, of course, Mrs Banda. She was so kind to them that for a long time they assumed that she was their mother. She had looked after them since they were only a few weeks old so it wasn't surprising that she had a soft spot for the twins. Of course, she looked after all the other children too, but Loveness and John always knew they were her favourites, especially John. Like so many women, Mrs Banda felt that because he was a boy, he was somehow better.

Every school holiday their father would come and fetch them, and on the bus going home they clamoured for his attention, both talking at once, wanting to tell him everything that had happened since they last saw him. Loveness worshipped her father, a feeling she never lost, although it was rarely apparent in her actions. She valued his qualities of loyalty and concern and saw that he did his best to make up for their mother's absence. He did such a good job that they were never conscious of missing anything. He was always there for them and while they were at home he would take leave, and they would embark on great journeys together with his elder daughter, Nancy, to Great Zimbabwe, to the game parks, to other towns. When they returned home after these trips, Mr Mukafa would sit down with them and go over all the things they had seen and done. He made learning fun and they seemed to spend much of their time together laughing.

But then Mr Mukafa decided to remarry. Perhaps he did it for himself or perhaps for the sake of his children. Maybe he thought that with two daughters, a woman's touch was needed, or maybe he was just lonely.

The twins were about seven when Mrs Banda called them into her room and told them that they were going to go home, for good this time, not just for a holiday. They were too excited at the idea of a permanent holiday, for that was what being with their father meant to them, to see the sadness in their surrogate mother's face; next day, when their father came to fetch them, they didn't notice the tears sparkle in her eyes as she waved them goodbye.

The bus journey was much as usual. It wasn't until they were walking to the house that their father told them he was going to get a new wife. He didn't refer to her as their mother; he just said that she'd be there to look after them whenever they weren't at school, and Nancy would be there too. She was three years older and had been living with an aunt in Harare while Loveness and John were at the orphanage.

By the time their stepmother appeared on the scene, they had already begun going to a primary school near their father's workplace and they would walk there together every morning.

Whatever the reason for the marriage, the children's lives now took a serious turn for the worse. Their new stepmother was very mean to them and made them sit in the yard when they weren't at school and unless her husband was around she refused to give them food.

'You're not my children. Why should I have to look after you? I have enough work and you do nothing but eat up your father's money. What is there left for me? Eh?' she would scream at them if they dared ask her for anything. They took to waiting for her to leave the house and then they would sneak into the cooking hut to eat the crusts from the *sadza* pot or any other scraps they could find. In time, the family's chickens were the scrawniest in the compound, for they never found any pickings. The children had eaten them all. Nancy, who had quickly understood the way things were going insisted her father send her to boarding school and within a few short months the twins were alone with their stepmother. Often the step mother would rant and rave about how hard life was for her, how without a man, a woman was nothing, and how it was a disgrace that their father wasted money educating two daughters who were going to leave him to look after some other man who would gain the benefit of his wealth.

When her own first child was born and it was a girl, she was very bitter. They often heard her muttering as she fed the child, 'Useless, useless. What good are you? Withering up my breasts, taking my nourishment. And for what? When I am old, you will be taken up with your husband. You will look after some other parents in their age. And me? Who will care for me? Useless.' She wanted to call the child Munyaradzi but Mr Mukafa refused.

'No,' he said, gazing tenderly at the ugly wrinkled little thing, 'the child must be called Rudo, because she was born of love.'

Loveness looked at her father in wonderment. How could he say this? Was it possible that he loved this woman, who at best ignored his children by his first marriage and beat them when she could? Perhaps it was then that Loveness began to withdraw her love and respect for her father, to grow into herself, instead of outwards, embracing life.

So Rudo the child became, and at last her stepmother had found a use for Loveness. It was she who carried Rudo around on her back until the child screamed to be fed. She was weaned as fast as her mother could manage it, so that Loveness could take over looking after her. She told her husband that she had no milk, but Loveness saw her binding her breasts so that he would not see the milk that dripped from them.

John and Loveness tried to tell their father about his wife, about how unkind she was but he wouldn't believe them. When he was around she was always smiling and pleasant, asking John if he had enough food – and of course he never had! He developed the habit of asking for more, and then hiding what he could, then next morning he and Loveness would sneak out of the village and eat it for breakfast.

Throughout this confusing time, Loveness's one solace was school. Every day there, she escaped the drudgery and misery of her home life by sinking into a different world. Her teachers were fond of her for she was bright and inquisitive and did her best to please them. In the evenings her father would go over her homework with her and she grew hot with pleasure at his attention, but even that was to change as he became more and more taken up with Rudo and later, Tungamirai, leaving Loveness feeling beached and rejected.

A second child was born not long after the first, and this one was a boy. The stepmother beamed with pride, and treated him like a small god. Loveness was never allowed to touch him although her care had been quite good for Rudo.

Life continued this way for about a year, and then during the school holidays, the children began to notice that their stepmother was even more irritable with them than usual, but they could not work out the reason. They had done nothing more or less than they ever did to earn her displeasure. Then one morning, she left Tungamirai with them and left the township. She was gone some time, and they began to be anxious for her return for Tunga was an awkward child, used to his mother's presence: he cried almost the whole time she was gone, except for short breaks when he had exhausted himself and fallen asleep. When their stepmother came back, John and Loveness were astonished to see her smiling and content, although she scolded Loveness about the tear streaks on her darling's cheeks.

This pattern continued throughout the holidays, until John became suspicious.

'What is it that she goes away for every few days? Do you

think our father knows about this? What can she be doing?' and he resolved to follow her.

Next morning, their stepmother got up, irritable as usual, and they guessed that by about ten o'clock she was going to leave Tunga behind, and go away. They were right. She left the village walking briskly, and Loveness and John followed her. By now Tunga was used to being with them, and he lay quietly on Loveness' back. They stayed well behind, for it was the dry season and there was little bush for them to hide behind. Also they could not be sure that Tunga would not wake up and call their presence to her attention. Shortly, their stepmother came to another village some distance from their own and they saw her go into one of the compounds.

'Maybe she's going to a *n'anga* for some *muti* to put on us,' whispered John, his eyes wide with fear.

'You follow her,' said Loveness, 'I'll wait here with Tunga. She could see he was scared, but she had to know what it was that made her stepmother change her personality from one minute to the next.

Ten minutes later John was back, lying breathless in the dust beside her.

'Well?' she demanded, but he was speechless, spluttering with wild embarrassed laughter.

'What is it?' Loveness whispered to him again, squeezing his arm. He squirmed out of reach, and before she knew it, he had taken off back the way they had come. Loveness took one look at the silent village behind them and followed. He was waiting for her on the main road but by now, his hilarity had taken on another hue. He looked chastened and a little unsure of himself.

'What is it?' she said again, crossly this time. She was regretting ever having sent him by himself. She glared at him and he looked back. At last he said, 'There's a man in there.'

'What sort of man?' asked Loveness, for she still had an idea that what was afoot was some sort of witchcraft, but it was much worse than that.

'She's in there with a man. They're lying together on the bed, laughing,' her brother at last managed, his face hot with embarrassment. Loveness couldn't believe it.

'What?' she shouted.

'They're, you know,' he said squirming in mortification.

'Oh, you are useless. What are you talking about!' she said in frustration, for although she knew perfectly well what he was getting at, she couldn't believe it. How could that horrible woman treat their wonderful father like that?

John looked straight at Loveness saying, 'You're the one who's being stupid. They're lying together on the bed, and they haven't got any clothes on,' he said, pronouncing each word very slowly and clearly.

'Do you think we should tell father?' asked Loveness as they walked disconsolately back home.

'He'd never believe us anyway. Has he ever believed us when we tell him how badly she treats us?'

It was true. It was as though their father had a blind spot where his wife was concerned. He would believe no wrong of her. He would simply think they were jealous.

By the time she was due to go to secondary school, Loveness was anxious to go as far away as possible from her stepmother and when she won a place at a prestigious convent school in Bulawayo, she was delighted. Her happiness was only marred by the fact that John, less academically bright than she, would be going to the local secondary school and so would be forced to remain within their stepmother's orbit.

Over the last year, Loveness had begun to feel more and

more critical of her father. Why couldn't he see that their stepmother hated her and John? Why did he care more for Rudo and Tungamirai than he did for them? In this, Loveness misjudged her father. He was genuinely fond of young children, but sometimes, he found himself comparing these two little ones unfavourably with the twins and then he favoured them more to make up for his lack of real feeling. When Loveness's scholarship came through, her father's pride knew no bounds. Now let them criticise, all those who had said he was wasting money educating a girl. For once, Loveness was the centre of attention and even her stepmother had to congratulate her. As she boarded the bus to her new life, her father stood proudly by her side.

At first, it was all new and exciting, but before long she began to miss her family. She hated the long nights in the dormitory with all the other girls. She forgot that it was she who had wanted to leave home, and began to blame her father for making her go away. It was his fault that she was so lonely here amongst strangers, and though she was filled with loneliness she determined that no one else would ever know.

On top of that there was the strangeness of attending Catholic school. Her father had never bothered much with religion but sometimes they went together to the Methodist church in the town. The rules and rituals of Catholicism were alien to her and the older nuns frightened her – she scented death and decay off them. Her only contact with her family was through her aunt, who had attended the school in her youth. With his new family responsibilities her father left it up to his sister to play the role of parent with the school and in her loneliness, Loveness imagined that her father wanted to get rid of her all together.

Even her schoolwork no longer satisfied her. The classes were large, and the nuns had no time to pay her special attention. Since she was much brighter than most of the other girls in her class she was often bored. Being cooped up in school all day, and then the chores afterwards – weeding the vegetable garden, helping in the kitchen – was all so dull that she began to long for the freedom she had known in the evenings at home when school was over.

She began to look longingly at the life outside the convent. Bulawayo was a big city, and the few glimpses she had of it made her resent the convent's restrictions even more. She had also begun to notice boys as something more than just an irritation. At last she found Edna, another girl who suffered in much the same way, and who also resented attending a strict convent school. The two were already established as best friends before Loveness understood that Edna's need to rebel was of a different order to her own. They spent much of their time working out new ways of avoiding doing as they were told.

In time they terrorised not only their classmates but even some of the teachers. What else was there for them to do? During the whole of the second and third terms they handed in only five pieces of homework, finding increasingly unlikely excuses for failing to submit them. On one memorable occasion they even burned all the other girls' exercise books so that they wouldn't be the only two who didn't hand in their science homework. Although Loveness didn't agree with this plan of Edna's, some stubborn streak prevented her from backing out in the face of her friend's scorn, but as she watched the exercise books burn she knew with a feeling of helplessness that this was the end of something. They couldn't possibly get away with this. The nuns were faced with a difficult problem.

They recognised that Edna was a bad influence on Loveness but they wanted Loveness to admit it herself. They called in her aunt in the hope that she might be able to talk some sense into her niece. Sitting opposite the older woman, Loveness longed to pour out the truth, to tell her about her stepmother and her own confusion, that it was not the real Loveness who was doing all these terrible things. But she knew her aunt would never believe her so she kept silent.

The next few weeks saw no improvement in the behaviour of the two girls and eventually in despair, the nuns were forced to expel them.

Loveness had anticipated this and so before the end of term, she wrote to her father telling him how much she hated the school, and how she was tired of being away from her family and as she wrote she saw that it was true. The unruly girl at the convent was a stranger to her and she longed for the old Loveness to come back. She begged her father to let her come home, and finish her secondary education at the same school in Redcliff as her brother John.

Of course, her father was unable to resist her plea and made the necessary arrangements for her to transfer. At the end of the term when the headmistress called her in to the office to tell her that she was unable to accept Loveness back at the convent the following term, Loveness replied with failing bravado, 'I've already arranged to go to Redcliff next year!' and bursting into tears, ran out of the office, leaving the nun shaking her head and wondering what on earth would become of the girl.

Loveness's father was now working at Zisco Steel, and had been promoted to shop foreman of the motor maintenance section. At last he was getting somewhere. But although Loveness was glad to find herself back with her family, she found it hard to change the habits she had developed while under Edna's influence. Each time she looked at her father's second family, she remembered his 'betrayal' in abandoning herself and John to their stepmother. School just didn't seem important anymore and she continued to feel alienated and unhappy. The only subject in which Loveness was at all interested was fashion and fabrics, and she would sometimes make clothes for herself or for Nancy.

Her father was busy with his new job and if he noticed that she rarely did any homework or who her friends were, he didn't say anything. Loveness and John had also grown apart over the year she spent at the convent and she found no comfort in his proximity. John had every intention of following in his father's footsteps and becoming a motor mechanic so he spent most of his spare time down at the plant watching the men as they went about their work, while Loveness hung around with a group of school dropouts, talking about boys and dreaming about getting married. In class, she sat with her friend Chipo, and they would doodle o their exercise books, staring out of the window willing the time to pass till they could join their friends who were free to spend their days as they chose. Every day, Loveness grew more and more resentful of the school uniform which made her look so childish, and the time she was forced to spend there when she could have been with her friends. As the terms ground slowly on, she grew more and more frustrated, hating everything, knowing the only reason for being there was to please her father, but not understanding why she still wanted to please him after all she felt he had done to her. If Solomon had had any idea what his daughter was feeling perhaps he could have found a way to help her, but his second wife was a barrier between them and by the time she was gone it was too late for him to salvage his relationship with Loveness.

It was the year before Loveness was to sit her O-Levels that her father finally discovered the truth about his wife. One day, he visited one of the outlying workshops unexpectedly, and finding it deserted took a walk to the nearby compound to see if the mechanic was there. As he neared the gate he saw the man coming out of one of the houses, his arm around a heavily pregnant woman. She was smiling up at him, and as she turned her head to see who was approaching the smile froze on her face. It was his wife.

Solomon was speechless with fury. All his children's complaints about this woman rang in his head and half blind with anger, he rushed at her. The mechanic pulled him off. Struggling, they fell to the ground. Finally Solomon freed himself and stood up, brushing the dirt from his clothes and wiping a trickle of blood from his nose.

'You witch!' he spat at his wife. 'You get yourself and your children out of my home this day. Now! And don't ever let me see you there again or I swear I'll kill you. And you!' he turned his venom on the mechanic, who was still crouching on the ground. 'You're out of a job as of now. I believe you were supposed to be working on the number six truck this morning, not whoring around on the company's time. Clear your things out. Now!' He turned his back on them and headed back to the pick-up, disappearing in a storm of dust.

When Loveness and John returned from school, they found the house strangely quiet and empty. It didn't take long to establish that all their stepsister's clothes had gone, and a little more adventurous investigation revealed that their stepmother's clothes were also gone. They were mystified, and their curiosity was not satisfied by their father. When he returned from work much later than usual, they could smell beer on his breath, cause for even further mystification because he very seldom drank.

As Loveness placed his plate of *sadza* in front of him he said, 'Your stepmother and sister and brother have left this place. They will not be back. I do not want to hear her name mentioned in this house again.'

Loveness managed to get some idea of what had happened out of her half-sister who was in first form at the school. Their father continued to pay their fees and to pay some maintenance for the children, but the woman and the mechanic left Redcliff that day and they never saw her again.

After their stepmother's departure, their father became withdrawn and less directly interested in how his children spent their time. It was easier than ever for Loveness to spend time with her drop-out friends, doing as little schoolwork as possible. With a little effort on her father's side, something of their relationship might still have been retrieved, but Mr Mukafa was not a man to discuss his disappointment in his wife with his daughter, and the gulf between them widened further.

In another year her O-Levels would be over and Loveness would be free from school forever. Free to begin her *real* life, which she was convinced could only happen when a man picked her up and made her into *someone*, his Wife. Not that she thought of it quite like that, for she had only the haziest idea about what the future could hold and even less idea that she herself could be an actor in it. All her life, things had happened *to* her; life was something that happened, not something she needed to make decisions about and by the time she understood better, it was almost too late.

When the O-Level results came out, Loveness was not surprised to find that she had failed every single subject. For her father it was a bombshell, but Loveness felt nothing. She had done as he wanted and stayed in school and now it was time to do something for herself. But it was Chipo's urgings that made her want to get away from home and go to the city.

'Let's have some fun Nessy!' she had pleaded. 'Now that we're out of that lousy school, let's live!'

Chipo had also failed her O-Levels, but in her case it was due to inability.

So Loveness told her father that she wanted to take up a course in dressmaking and design and to do so she would have to go to Harare. She felt only a small twinge of guilt, which she easily suppressed when she saw how happy he was to give her the money.

'Good girl,' he'd said. 'Do something to improve yourself so that I needn't think I did a bad job of bringing you up.'

The aunt with whom Nancy had stayed while Loveness and her brother were at the orphanage was still in Harare and she agreed to have Loveness to live with her. Her father gave her the fees for the course, instructions to buy some items for the house in Redcliff and some pocket money, and Loveness arrived in the capital city. She soon met up with Chipo, and the two girls spent their days wandering about to and from the shops, sometimes taking the bus into town and window shopping.

Chapter Four

Just a few weeks after her arrival in the city, Loveness met Roderick, who was spending some time at his sister's place in Mufakose. Whenever the strain of being Doctor Baker's tame HIV boy became too great, Roderick would plead family business and go and stay with his mother for a while. Then when he needed more money, he would return to Doctor Baker's and go around on some school visits. He'd already become quite comfortable living a double life, pretending to be the good African boy with Doctor Baker and the Centre people, although he sometimes rebelled internally over the role he had created for himself. He could not afford to get drunk at Doctor Baker's, or to take a woman there. A slip like that could ruin everything, so he would stay in Mufakose when he needed to drink, or when he wanted to look for a woman.

Roderick and his drinking companions were passing the time standing on the *stoep* outside the bottle store when the two young girls walked slowly past them and into the dark interior. Roderick noticed Loveness straight away. She had that look of innocent provocation that he knew said 'virgin' and that was how he liked them best. That way they were sure to fall in love with you and believe every word you said, and he needed that sort of dependence – it reminded him of his complete omnipotence as a child, before his father had died and everything had changed.

The two girls came out of the store and walked slowly along the dusty street.

'What do you think of that one?' asked one of Roderick's cronies, seeing his long stare at the retreating back.

'Mmmmm. Juicy,' he replied, watching the swaying hips, admiring the neat waist. 'Who is she? I don't remember seeing her around here before.'

'She's Chipo's friend,' answered one of the others. 'She's supposed to be here to study I think, but I haven't seen her go anywhere.'

'Huh,' interrupted Roderick, 'what's the point of a girl studying anyway. She looks old enough to be doing something more useful with herself,' he leered, and the others laughed appreciatively.

Loveness had not missed the handsome young man either and over the next few weeks, they began to greet each other, stopping to chat for a few minutes. It was when she felt her heart quicken at the sight of him, that Loveness knew she was in love with the man.

One evening, she and Chipo were walking together when they came across Roderick and his friends. By now, Loveness was so dazzled by the attention he showed her that she couldn't even speak to him. As he teased and flattered her she hung her head and looked at the ground, feeling her face grow hot and unable to think of anything to say. Chipo didn't seem to have any such problems. She was sparkling under the attention, chattering, teasing and laughing with the others who were leading her away while Roderick hung behind.

'You don't want to go with them, do you?' he teased her, and took Loveness's arm. 'I know somewhere quiet we can go. Just the two of us. You'd like that wouldn't you?'

She nodded dumbly and her feet moved one in front of the other, her heart singing and at the same time tense with anticipation and nerves. He liked her. He had noticed her. This was what she'd dreamed of – meeting a man, not a boy, and knowing instantly that this was what she was made for, to be his wife, to look after him. Here was her destiny. He was what she had dreamed of. Here, at last, was life.

Years later when she first told others her story, her voice filled with irony as she said these words.

'My destiny', she said, 'I really did meet my destiny, didn't I?' as tears spilled down her cheeks.

Within days of their first kiss Roddy was telling her how beautiful she was and soon he began talking of marriage.

'I love you, Loveness. We'll get married and live together in our own house, and I'll go out to work while you stay at home and keep house for me. And we'll have at least three beautiful children!'

She had never been attracted to boys of her own age. They all reminded her too much of her twin brother and she thought there was nothing admirable about him! But Roderick was considerably older than her and she was thrilled by the idea of his experience, by the thought that she, young as she was, could attract a man of his age and obvious sophistication. So, the more Loveness saw of the man at the bottle store, the more in love she became with her idea of him. She was completely taken in by his sweet talk. But then she had no reason to doubt what he said, to mistrust the candied words that he spoke with such ease, and she had no armour at all against the language of her own body when he held her in his arms and she felt desire grow in him.

She had really known very few men or boys apart from her

father and brother, and if her father had a fault, it was that he was too willing to let his women folk have their own way. Even when his second wife had taken a lover, he had not beaten her or remonstrated with her. She had merely disappeared from their lives. Roderick was what she'd dreamed of all those long days in school, staring out of the window at the playground. Daydreams that were fuelled by night time gossip in the dormitory when they fantasised about all those things the nuns forbade them to even think about – about finding a man as handsome and responsible as her father, though, of course, in her dreams her man would never let her down.

She was much too in love to wonder how Roderick supported himself, to wonder why he didn't seem to have a job. She believed she loved him totally, despite the fact that she knew so little about him, had never met any of his family, nor he hers. Every single minute that she wasn't with him, she thought about him; she thrilled at the thought of the things he said, at the idea of his caresses, at the imagining of the beautiful children they would have together. More and more, they wandered off together, leaving Chipo and the others. Sometimes he would accidentally touch her breast. She would brush his hand away, while secretly wanting to press it to her, to feel her body melt into his. But they had nowhere private to go and she refused to allow him to do more than kiss her.

'Why don't you come and see me at home, and meet my aunt?' she urged him, wanting to formalise their relationship, have it sanctioned by her family. 'I'm sure they'll like you and then we'll be able to see more of each other,' for she was still forced to return home early in the evenings, lest she arouse her aunt's suspicions.

But Roderick always evaded these invitations. He had no intention of going to meet her family, just as he had no intention of marrying her. He knew it wouldn't be long before she gave in and once that happened she would make no further difficulties for him. He had other reasons for not wanting to meet her family too. He was afraid that they might remember him from the *Tribune* photo.

Over the weeks and months since Roderick had found out about his infection he wavered constantly between disbelief about the virus and its effects, and occasional, absolute despair. He had never lived long without a woman of some sort to care for him and now, since his appearance in the paper, he could not hope to go back to any of his previous wives for they would all have heard the story. Loveness appealed to him because she was so clearly besotted with him. She was too young to stand up to him and he could see she was the kind of girl who would submit completely to her husband's will. So he set about the task of snaring her as he would a wild animal, with great care and with caution. He knew there were dangers in what he planned to do, but what alternative did he have? He needed a woman. He needed someone to love him and look after him and Loveness had offered herself up to him.

For a further two months, Loveness resisted Roderick's advances. Each day she would leave her aunt's house in the morning and return home again in the evening so that it would look as though she were attending classes, but Roderick was becoming impatient. He was a man with strong sexual desires, used to getting what he wanted, and he badly wanted to taste the sweetness of Loveness's youthful flesh. She was unexpectedly prudish about allowing his embraces and he was beginning to get anxious that something would go wrong with his plan. So many things could happen: they might bump into her aunt or some other relative and he would be recognised; her family would discover she wasn't attending classes; some irate father would come and drag her away. Perhaps Doctor Baker would come looking for him and let something out, or Loveness herself might insist on marriage. The possibilities were endless. He had to move quickly.

One evening, he persuaded her to tell her aunt that she would be going to the cinema with Chipo and would be back late. He wanted to take her home to meet his family he told her, but he already knew that there would be no one home that evening because they were all going *kumusha* to brew beer that weekend. He couldn't risk taking her straight to Doctor Baker's – as far as she knew, he lived in Mufakose at his sister's. No. He needed to be sure that she wouldn't make a fuss, that she would stay, before he tried taking her there.

They arrived at the house in Mufakose early, and he pretended to wonder why there was no one there. He had told her he wanted her visit to be a surprise.

'There's always someone here by this time, I can't understand it,' he said. 'Anyway, sit down. I'm sure there'll be someone here soon.' He sat her down on the sofa, and then went into the kitchen where he pulled out a bottle of *Don Juan*, a glass and a bottle of beer for himself. Loveness looked up in surprise when she saw what he carried.

'I thought we should celebrate, my lovely one!' he said, as he sat beside her and put the glasses on the table. 'After all, it's not every day I bring my future wife home to meet my family!' he poured a healthy measure of the sweet sherry into the glass and handed it to her. Then he opened his own bottle of beer and chinking it against her glass he urged her to drink, saying: 'To us!'

Tentatively, Loveness sipped the liquid in the glass. She had never tasted anything alcoholic before and did not know what to expect but it was sweet, with a strange aftertaste. She swallowed it and savoured the warmth it left in her mouth.

'It's good, isn't it?' said Roderick, smiling at the look on her face,

'Ye-s,' she replied doubtfully.

'Take another sip. It'll taste better the second time,' and so she did and she found that he was right. Soon she felt warm all over.

As they sat in the softly growing darkness and the night grew loud with the sounds of crickets Roderick put his arm around her and kissed her softly and hesitantly on the lips. He heard, felt her catch her breath against his mouth, and pulled back a little until she herself sought out his lips again. He touched her breast but immediately she pulled back and he held her away from him.

'What's wrong, my sweet?' he said so innocently, so tenderly, that Loveness felt she had accused him of some unpleasant intention even though she had said nothing and she turned her head against his neck.

'Nothing Roderick. It's just...' but she was too shy to tell him her fears, to speak openly and taking advantage of her hesitation, he pulled her closer.

'I love you my darling Loveness. I could never do anything to hurt you. I want to be with you, I want to love you,' and gently he pulled her face back so that she was looking into his eyes.

'Don't you love me, Loveness? Don't you want to be my wife?'

'Oh, Roderick, I want it more than anything else in the world,' she said with such longing in her voice that he knew he had won.

'Then trust me sweetie, trust me,' but he sensed her tension still. She was like a nervous buck, ready to bolt if he pushed her too far so after a while, when he could feel she had begun to enjoy his kisses, he pulled away, and poured her some more sherry. He fetched himself another beer.

'You know, my family might come home at any minute. Why don't we go to my place in town?'

It was a calculated risk to stop now, but he knew they had to go elsewhere if his seduction was to succeed. Any minute now she would protest that they might be interrupted and he could hardly admit that no one would be coming.

'Your place in town? But I thought you lived here in Mufakose.'

He bit his lip in annoyance at the thought that she might now say no, she had better go home. So near and yet so far. But he answered mildly, 'It's only you that's kept me in Mufakose all this time, my sweet. No, I have a room in town, at the back of an old doctor's house. I work for him sometimes and that's where I stay.'

In one sentence he had answered her remaining question – if he had his own place how did he support himself? With the newfound confidence given by the sherry she was eager to see the place her beloved lived in. As they left the house Roderick slipped the rest of the sherry and another beer into a bag, and they caught the bus to town.

His one last concern now was that they would somehow bump into Doctor Baker, but their journey was uneventful and when they arrived at the gate of the old house it was in darkness. He breathed a sigh of relief and led Loveness down the garden path and into his room. He switched on the light and she walked ahead of him into the small, comfortable lodging and sat on the solitary chair. He let this pass and busied himself with setting down the glasses and smoothing out the bed. It was a pleasant room, and the light from the lamp cast a warm cosy glow over the two of them.

'Are you hungry?' he asked her, praying that she would say no.

'No. Can I have another drink?' this was better than he could ever have hoped.

'Are you sure you should?' he said, not daring to push his luck. One more drink and she would be his for sure.

But Roderick need not have worried. When Loveness had heard that he had a place of his own and had agreed to come and see it she had already made her decision: she knew that she wouldn't be going home again. Tonight she would be truly his, forever. Another drink would just make it easier for her to take the final step.

He poured the drink and she sipped it still sitting on the edge of the chair.

'Are you afraid of me? Is that why you're sitting there where I can't touch you?' he teased her.

She giggled, and he sat on the bed, patting the space beside him. As she made to sit he pulled her to one side, so that she lay across the bed. He lay beside her and heard her sigh. He turned her face towards him, kissing her long and deep. She moaned softly against his chest. Her body was soft and warm, trusting even, and he knew he could teach her to be a good lover. Afterwards, he raised himself on his elbows and looked at her. Her cheeks were wet.

'What is it, Loveness?' did I hurt you?'

'No. It was nice. I just love you, that's all,' and he felt the rush of triumph, like a drug surging through his blood. He had done it. She would never leave him now, whatever happened.

And there he was almost right.

Loveness didn't go home to her aunt's that night, or

indeed ever again. The next day she waited till she knew everyone would be out and slipped into the house, packed her things, and moved in with Roderick.

Chapter Five

When Loveness failed to turn up that evening her aunt was very worried, but at the same time she was not surprised. Ever since the girl had come she had sensed things were not as they seemed. Now that intuition deepened into certainty. After two days, she went to the college where Loveness had told her she was studying. It was no revelation to find that they had never heard of the girl. It was as if she had known even before she went there that it had all been a lie. On her way home she went to Chipo's house to see if she might know where Loveness had gone, but Chipo protested with an innocence the aunt could not believe and she returned home knowing no more than before.

'Poor Solomon,' she sighed to herself, thinking of her brother and the misfortunes he had suffered, 'I always knew the girl would come to no good, and he has tried so hard.' She pondered the situation for another few days, not wanting to alarm her brother, and hoping she would find out where Loveness had gone but no one seemed to know anything. After a week of fruitless enquiries she decided to go and tell Solomon herself. The more she thought about Loveness the angrier she grew at the girl's lack of gratitude for all the opportunities she had been given, for the pain this latest news would cause her brother. She also felt a little guilty, for she knew she hadn't tried very hard to find out what was wrong with Loveness, why she had so suddenly wanted to leave home and had behaved so badly at the convent. The aunt had always compared Loveness unfavourably with Nancy, even when they were children. Loveness lacked the qualities that were admired in a girl: humility and circumspection. She was too clever for her own good. Nancy, now, there was a good girl. Clever in her own way, but quiet, never forward or cheeky, always looking for something she could do to help. By the time she arrived in Redcliff, she had convinced herself that the only thing to do was to let the girl go her own way. That was what she would tell Solomon.

She was waiting for him when he arrived back from work. Her brother's face lifted when he saw her, but then seeing from her expression that this was not a social visit, he immediately became concerned.

'What is it *Sisi*? What brings you all this way?'

'Brother, I did not want to write with worrying news. It's Loveness. When I returned from work last Thursday, I found no sign of her, and she didn't come home that night. The maid says that when she came in the afternoon, she found Loveness's things all gone from the cupboard, but she did not see her. I have spent this last week trying to find some trace of her, but you know Harare is a big place...'

Solomon stared at her uncomprehendingly and she couldn't bear to see the disappointment dawning on his face.

The twins had been all the more dear to him because their mother had died giving birth to them. Now he could only blame himself for what had happened to Loveness. She had been a lovely child but once she began to go to secondary school she had changed, grown hard and selfish. Part of the problem was that she was too bright for her own good. She was bored at school, and she seemed to have a knack for becoming friends with girls who had aptitude only for mischief.

Sisi had known about the nuns' intention to expel her niece, for she had attended the school herself and knew the nuns well. They had called her to ask advice about Loveness, but though she had tried to talk to the girl she didn't seem able to make contact with her. She had told no one about the expulsion. Solomon had enough to worry about and what good could it do? Then when her brother had wanted to send Loveness to her in Harare she had hoped that maybe living together she would get to know her and be able to influence her. But she hadn't stayed long enough for that. Having made this journey she was now determined to make her brother see that he must forget about Loveness for she had taken herself beyond their influence.

'You mustn't blame yourself for Loveness,' she said to her brother. 'She's always been wayward, and you've given her everything a girl could possibly ask for. My advice is that you forget her now. No doubt if she's in trouble she'll come looking for us, but that one can look after herself.'

Shocked at the bitterness in his sister's voice, Solomon could only remember the bright laughing face of the child he had collected from the orphanage all those years ago, the eager questions, the laughter. What had happened to her? Why did she treat him like this?

'My sister, why do you sound so bitter. What has happened?'

Sisi was prepared to tell him everything, if it would only make him forget, and stop blaming himself.

'There's something I want to tell you. I never told you before because I didn't think it would help. You remember when Loveness told you she wanted to leave the convent because she was homesick and wanted to be at home?'

'Yes,' he replied, 'but that was long ago.'

'Well, it wasn't true. She knew they were going to expel her so she wrote to you first, so that you wouldn't have to find out.'

Solomon was stunned.

'But why? Why were they going to expel her?'

'Because she and one of her friends were disrupting the whole school. They teased the older nuns, burned the other girls' exercise books, never did any homework and generally did their best to be a nuisance.'

'I don't understand. Why should she behave like that?'

'I don't know Solomon, she just did. It's not your fault – she's a silly, selfish child. I didn't want to tell you because I didn't think it would make any difference. I tried talking to her but she wouldn't even listen to me and you had your heart set on her doing her O-Levels – you wouldn't have believed me if I'd told you you were wasting your money...'

'No,' said Solomon slowly, 'I don't suppose I would have. She's such a different child from the others. But she's so bright. Why should she waste the chances she had?' he shook his head.

'I don't think she recognised the chances, Solomon. It all came too easily to her.' Solomon grunted his disagreement.

'How can you say that, *Sisi*? Those poor children lost their mother before they even had time to know her. She and John were in that orphanage for seven years. But there was nothing else I could do.'

'As I said, it's not your fault, brother. Look at John! He was in the orphanage too, and you couldn't ask for a better son. He may not be bright for schoolwork, but I'm sure he's going to be a good man. And Nancy. There's nothing wrong with her either. It's just Loveness. It's her choice. She's made her decision about how she wants to live and you've given her all you can. Let her go now, or she'll only hurt you more.'

Solomon shook his head, staring into the fire; a picture of his second wife came into his mind, and he knew that *sisi* was right. His heart quailed at the thought that Loveness might be like her, but he had enough to worry about, with Nancy and John and maintenance to pay for the two from his second wife. He would put Loveness aside, as she had done him.

'You're right, *sisi*. I have no daughter Loveness anymore. Until she chooses to claim her family, she is gone from us.'

Loveness and Roderick had been living together for two weeks before she met Doctor Baker and he greeted her kindly and very gently, she thought. It was only much later that she understood that the good doctor had appreciated a great deal more about her situation than she had herself. A young woman, little more than a child, whose life was to be over such a short time after it had begun.

Not long after, Doctor Baker had called Roderick up to the house for a pep talk, stimulated no doubt by Loveness's evident youthfulness.

'Ah, Roderick, come in, come in,' the doctor called heartily when he heard Roderick's footsteps. Roderick came quietly into the study and stood by the doctor's desk.

'What's this I hear about you having company down there, boy.'

'Oh that, doctor. I've been meaning to talk to you about her. She is Loveness. I met her at the AWC. She's an HIV girl. Her boyfriend died some months back and she'd gone there for help. She recognised me from my picture in the paper.' The lies came out so easily, the story they told so plausible. Doctor Baker never dreamed it might not be the truth.

'Ah, I see. She's very young, isn't she? Shame.'

Roderick stood there awkwardly. There was never anything he could say when the doctor began to go on about young lives cut off in their prime.

'Well now, that's all right then,' the doctor said briskly. 'I just wanted to make sure you know what you are doing. Using condoms, aren't you? You must know, even if she's already infected. Better for both of you.'

'Oh yes doctor, of course.'

The doctor said goodnight, and Roderick escaped down the garden, flooded with relief. That was it then, all sorted out.

Loveness was preparing supper, and gave him her usual dazzling smile when he came in. She was still brimming with the splendour of being Roderick's woman – no matter that he hadn't mentioned the marriage again. For the time being she was supremely happy, confident that the future held only good things.

That afternoon Doctor Baker came down to their room and gave Roderick a message from the nuns at Mbare. They wanted him to go and see them as soon as possible. This was it, thought Roderick. She had to learn some version of the truth sooner or later. It might as well be now.

'You must come with me Loveness. They'll want to meet you.'

'Why do you have to go there?'

'Oh, it's part of my work for Doctor Baker. You'll find out soon enough.' Roderick replied vaguely. He was banking on Loveness's blind willingness to accept anything he said and, as he intended, she asked him no further questions.

Together they arrived at the church hall in Mbare, where, to Loveness's surprise, Roderick seemed to be the star attraction. Everyone knew him; then one of the younger nuns took Loveness aside and began to talk to her, very kindly about dying and how she must prepare herself to meet the Lord even though she felt strong and healthy now. Loveness was puzzled, but thinking that perhaps they belonged to one of those strange religious groups, she just listened and nodded respectfully.

This went on for a couple of weeks, and slowly Loveness began to understand that it was all to do with a disease she had never heard of, which they called AIDS. She had barely even heard about sexually transmitted diseases before this and suddenly everyone seemed to be talking about this particular disease, about dying, and somehow she and Roderick were always at the centre of it. The first real note of disquiet came one day when she overheard the young nun, Sister Gabriella, who had first talked to her, questioning Roderick. They were sitting in a corner and she had a long questionnaire on a clipboard. She was writing down Roderick's answers to the questions. Loveness had to go over and interrupt them, and as she reached them she heard the nun ask, 'and what age did you say you are Roddy?'

'Thirty-two, sister. I'll be thirty-three in March.'

Loveness was shocked. Thirty-two! She had never imagined Roderick was so much older, why, he was twice her age. He was almost old enough to be her father! Later that night she wondered about it again. If Roderick was that old, he *must* have had a wife before. Perhaps still had. Perhaps that was why he'd stopped talking about marriage. Perhaps he had children too. Why hadn't he told her? But maybe she had always known it, for something stopped her from asking. The next time they went to Mbare the nuns gave them some blankets and food and at last she asked Roderick for an explanation.

'What is all this about, Roderick. Why are they giving us these things?'

'It's great, isn't it? You see how well we can live, and we don't even have to work.'

'But why, Roderick? Why are they treating us like this? The nuns make me feel so strange, like I'm special in some horrible way. They keep talking to me about dying.'

'Okay, okay, I'll explain. You must know about AIDS by now – they've been talking to you about it enough. Well, they think we've got it, that we're looking after us. It's a good bluff, isn't it?'

'But that's a terrible thing to do Roderick!' she wasn't convinced by his explanation. 'Is that what you've told Doctor Baker too?'

'That's it. You know sometimes I go away with him? Well, we go to schools and I talk about being infected with this virus, and he gives me money.'

'I see,' replied Loveness, but she didn't see, and a reluctant seed of doubt began to grow in her heart. Later when Roderick told her what she should tell the nuns, her doubt grew larger.

'Remember to tell them we met a while ago now, Ness, and that you found out because your boyfriend died. We both have to tell the same story.'

'All right. If you say so.' But she was deeply uneasy.

Later that week Roderick went off somewhere on his own and Loveness decided to go up to the main house and speak to Doctor Baker. She had to find out more about Roderick. The kind old man could see that she was nervous and afraid and told her to come in and sit down, talking away to try and help her relax. He knew she was very young, and just the sight of her and the knowledge that she was going to have her brief life cut short made anger boil up inside him, so he was at his gentlest with her and did his best to comfort her. He told her that now that she was infected she must accept it and just take care of herself, no smoking or drinking or taking any risks with her health, that she could avoid things like getting malaria.

'You're very young, and maybe they'll find a cure before you get sick,' he went on, 'You and Roderick must use condoms, you know, for your sake especially. We don't want you getting pregnant now do we? You could pass the infection on to your baby. But even without that, having sex without condoms exposes you to reinfection and other sexually transmitted diseases.' He looked at her kindly to check that she understood what he was saying.

Listening, Loveness wanted the ground to open up and swallow her. Did she really want to hear the answer to the question she had come here to ask? Was it possible that Roderick had fooled all these people into thinking he was infected? And besides, that very month she had missed her period. Roderick never used condoms. How often had she heard him say, 'No point in eating a sweet with the wrapper on.'

Pretending that she was making casual conversation she said,

'You've been such a help to us doctor. How did you come to meet Roderick?'

'Oh, the same place as you, my dear,' he replied, 'at the AIDS Welfare Centre. I work from there, you know. He'd been sent there from the clinic at the place where he used to work. One of the tragedies of this whole thing is that people lose their jobs, lose everything. He had nowhere to stay, lost his accommodation too. I offered him this place, and in return he helps us out, talking to schools and things. He's a very brave young man your Roderick. Actually volunteered to speak to *The Tribune* when they managed to infiltrate the HIV group. Did he ever show you the article? Gave him a few rough weeks that did.' As he spoke he moved towards the filing cabinet in the corner. Then he had a folder in his hand, and he opened it and showed it to her. There, staring at her, was Roderick and the headline: *HIV Positive Group aims to "live positively"* and she looked at the date. Just a few weeks before she had come to Harare.

'Good picture isn't it – couldn't get any of the others to identify themselves in public.' Doctor Baker said.

'Yes. Yes it is.' She couldn't stay there any longer. She had to be by herself, to think.

'Well, thanks, doctor. You, you've been very helpful. I, I must go now,' she stammered. The doctor was surprised at the sudden change in her composure, but then he had seen shock affect people in so many different ways with this thing – maybe she'd just realised she could lose Roderick too.

'Certainly, my dear, certainly. And remember I'm always here if you need someone to talk to.'

Running down the path to the servant's quarters, Loveness practically knocked down old Noah as he came out of the toilet but she pushed past him into their room and stood leaning against the closed door, her heart thumping and her mind absolutely blank.

She stood there like that for some time until her thoughts began to batter her senses, insisting on being heard. Roderick had lied to her. He *was* infected. He had to be. And he had infected her. Deliberately. He knew and he had infected her. But still her love for Roderick denied that her suspicions could be true.

It couldn't be true. She was being foolish. Roderick was always on the lookout for himself but he wasn't a bad person, wasn't he helping people by talking about HIV even if it wasn't true that he was infected? Then she roused herself and looked around the small home she had created for the two of them and her eyes were drawn towards the corner, to the small wooden chest in which she knew Roderick kept his personal papers. Like a sleepwalker she moved towards it and lifted the lid. On top were some photographs, she recognised what must be his mother and some of his sisters; there was one of Roderick with his arm around the shoulders of a pretty young woman, both of them laughing at the camera and underneath that she found a hospital form. At the sight of it she was bathed in a cold sweat. She stilled her panic enough to read the first few lines: 'In accordance with your recent blood test carried out at the national pathology laboratory we have to inform you that the test was positive for HIV.' She read it again. And again, her eyes taking in each letter lest there be some mistake, some difference between what her eyes were seeing and her mind was understanding. But there was none. Roderick had had an HIV test and he was positive. The date was two years earlier. He had known for that long and he had knowingly infected her. She slumped to the ground with her back against the bed, the paper in her hand and wept. It was too late now for her. She knew that from all the dummy counselling she had had from the nuns. There was nothing she could do to help herself. She was going to die.

It was two days before Roderick came back and she was able to confront him with what she had discovered. He tried to deny it, to tell her that she had got it all wrong until she went to the chest and took out the hospital form. Suddenly he began shouting and yelling at her. He pushed her against the wall.

'What do you think you're doing snooping about my things? You're not my wife. You have no business looking in my chest. From now on I'll keep it locked. What difference does it make if I've got this stupid infection anyway? We're alive aren't we?

We're living well on all these handouts. I'm not sick. It's not my fault. I never forced you to love me. You made your own choice. Did I bring AIDS to Zimbabwe? I was just unlucky. It's not my fault!' and he turned around and left the room, locking the door behind him.

Loveness was too stunned by his tirade to think anymore. What he said was true. He hadn't forced her in any way. She had made her own choice. She couldn't deal now with the rights and wrongs of it all. She could only think of how much she loved him, and how fierce he had seemed when he shouted at her, how hard he had pushed her against the wall and how afraid she was that he would hit her. And he had locked the door. Oddly she was comforted by that – it meant that he would come back.

For a long time she lay on the bed, sometimes trying to pray for the first time since she left the convent. Where had Roderick gone? He mustn't leave her now. She had given him her life. She couldn't lose him now. After a while she got up and began to prepare food hoping that the act alone might make him come back. She heard his key in the lock and jumped up to greet him. He entered looking surly and she threw her arms around him.

'Oh Roderick, I'm sorry. I'm sorry I looked in your box. I know it's not your fault, but I had to know. Tell me you forgive me.'

He put his arms around her and said, 'Is that food I smell?' and she pulled away from him and ran to bring him his supper.

The next two weeks were the worst Loveness had ever known. Roderick was sullen and resentful and she was torn by doubts and confusion. She loved him, but she couldn't get the fact of his infection out of her head. He had *knowingly* infected her. He had never even mentioned condoms and now she was quite sure she was pregnant. She would have to go to the clinic and find out. She felt as if her head was a canyon down which a raging torrent of thoughts surged, hitting blind walls and rushing madly on. And still she found no answers. Then one morning she awoke and her mind was suddenly still. She knew she must leave Roderick. She couldn't stay with him, not now that she was sure she was pregnant, and the way things were between them she couldn't tell him about it. She had to get away, but how? Roderick had taken to locking up her clothes when he went out and he had taken full responsibility for buying food so that she never had any money of her own.

For a month she watched for her chance, determined to go, and then Roderick announced that he had to go away for a few days. On the evening of the day he left, she went up to the main house to see Doctor Baker. She told him that there was a problem at home and Roderick had gone away and she didn't have enough money. Could he lend her something, just enough to go home? He gave her enough for her bus fare to Mufakose and she made her way back to her aunt's house. But when she got there, her aunt was away and only her uncle was there. He wasn't pleased to see her and grudgingly gave her enough money to get her to Redcliff.

'And make sure you go there,' was his parting shot.

Chapter Six

On the long bus journey Loveness stared out of the window wondering how much she could tell her father and how he would react. It didn't take her long to decide that she couldn't tell him the truth. She didn't even know why she was going home except that it was some instinctive need to be where she had once felt secure and loved. She still loved Roderick. She couldn't believe that he deliberately meant her harm, but she couldn't tell him about the baby. Not yet.

She couldn't tell her family about being HIV positive. They probably wouldn't even know what it was. She had never heard about it until Sister Gabriella had started talking to her about it. In any case she still hadn't taken it in herself. To tell someone else would somehow make it real. She was much too young to be able to understand something as awesome as the fact that she might be dying. She couldn't afford to understand something so final. Not yet.

So Loveness continued doing what she had done all her life. Living without thought, as passive as an animal in the bush. Waiting for life to come and get her. But it was death that had risen up out of the undergrowth to claim her for his own.

She arrived at the house in Redcliff about 4 o'clock and let herself in with the key that was kept under the flower pot by the step. Her father would be home soon. She wondered where John and Nancy had gone. It was strange to find the house empty. She began to be anxious about what she would say to her father, about what he would say to her. She supposed he would be angry but that, underneath it all, he would welcome her back, be glad to see her. She was quite aware that she had always been his favourite: that was one of the reasons she had felt it was possible to run away as she did. That, and the fact that her desire for some excitement and then her love for Roderick had seemed more important than anything else.

She heard his weary footsteps on the path and then the turn of his key in the lock. As he entered the room he looked at her in disbelief. A light crossed his face and was swiftly extinguished to be replaced by a frown.

'What's brought you back here? Why have you come back?'

It was far from being a welcome, but she had not expected to be accepted back like the prodigal son. Prodigal daughters were something quite different.

She found herself unable to say anything meaningful, and merely replied, 'I thought I should come and see you.'

He grunted, and they spent the evening in grudging silence. He asked her no more questions but when she asked him where her brother and sister where he replied, 'I can't see why it should trouble you where they are. You've been gone six months now and it never bothered you before.'

It was then that Loveness first glimpsed what had happened between herself and her father to cause such a gulf between them. She believed he had betrayed her and so she had hurt him in the only way she knew, but she saw that more than that, she had betrayed herself. She began to understand how much pain she had caused her father, and yet here she was, bringing more trouble upon him.

The following day an aunt arrived to talk to her. Her father must have realised that something was up. Reluctantly Loveness told the aunt that she was pregnant, but sensing the woman's disapproval added quickly, 'But the father wants to marry me.'

'Oh really?' replied her aunt harshly. 'If that is the truth then why have you run away from him?' she demanded. 'Has he thrown you out? No? Then go back to him, to the father of your child.' Each word was laden with scorn and disgust and Loveness despaired.

She had assumed she would speak to her father, not to some strange aunt, but she could tell them nothing more. There would be no help from that quarter.

Later, her father and aunt talked for some time and then her father came to speak to her. His face was full of pain. He held out a few dollars.

'I am told you have been spoiled. Tell your man if he has any decency he'll come and speak to your father about the damage he has caused, or to pay your lobola.'

'Father...' she began, but when she met his eyes the words died on her lips. She wanted to ask him for mercy, to ask him to look after her the way he had done when she was a child; but she had forfeited the right to comfort. She could see it in his eyes and kneeling she quietly clapped her hands and took the money he offered.

Early next morning she was on the bus back to Harare and for once she was forced to think ahead, to make decisions for herself. Her father had given her thirty dollars, more than he could afford, she thought, but it wouldn't last long. Where could she go, for she was still not prepared to go back to Roderick.

By the time the bus arrived at Mbare Musika she had at

least formulated a plan. She would find Sister Gabriella. She would surely find a way to help her. There was no one else. Sister Gabriella had to help her. The young nun had seemed to like her, and now that she genuinely needed help she needn't feel guilty about asking for it.

To her relief, Sister Gabriella was at the church hall, and as soon as she saw Loveness she sensed there was something wrong and took her aside. Faced with the sympathy she had longed for, Loveness broke down and as she sobbed she managed to tell the nun that she was pregnant and that her family had refused to take her in.

'Why, you poor child,' said the nun, 'but what about Roderick, dear. Where is he?'

'I don't know,' sobbed Loveness. 'I ran away when I found out I was pregnant. I don't think he'll like it. I don't want him to know,' she added, a note of desperation in her voice.

'All right dear, all right. Now calm down and we'll see what can be done. I've got to be here until about three-thirty, but then I'll be free and I can take you to the shelter we run for girls like you. I'm sure they'll be able to fit you in, at least for tonight. You sit down over here and wait for me. Everything will be all right. You'll see.'

And miraculously, it was all right. Loveness settled into the shelter and the weeks of her pregnancy were uneventful. No one mentioned Roderick. She even had an HIV test done and it was negative, although they warned her that it might not be a true result. As her time grew near, she found herself looking forward to the birth of her child, to having something of her own to love.

The baby was born just two days later than she was due, and it was a fine healthy baby boy. She decided to call him Solomon, after her father. She and the baby had been back at the shelter for two days when Roderick suddenly arrived with his mother. After a brief battle with her superior, Sister Gabriella had submitted to the older woman's belief that Roderick had a right to know about his child, and ignorant of the other problems between him and Loveness, told him where to find her. He greeted Loveness without emotion, but when he saw the bouncing baby boy she nursed he could not help a delighted grin breaking across his face.

'He's beautiful, Loveness. What a clever girl you are,' and he thought with wonder that Loveness, of all the women he had had, Loveness had actually given him a son.

The nuns were delighted when Roderick told them that Loveness and the baby would go home with him and his family. As far as they were concerned it was one of the few happy endings in the many miserable cases they had to deal with. Loveness's test was negative, the baby was thriving. Perhaps she was one of the lucky ones.

For three months, the relationship between Loveness and Roderick thrived along with their child. She managed to forget everything that had gone before, and Roderick was once again the charming, handsome man she had fallen in love with. But it was not to stay that way for long. The baby began to be sick. At first it was just a bad cough but they got some antibiotics from the clinic and he recovered. Then he developed thrush, but lots of babies had thrush. That too cleared up. The next was more serious. He had already failed to put on weight because of his earlier problems and then he developed a bad case of diarrhoea. When she noticed that his fontanelle had collapsed, Loveness took him straight to the hospital and they admitted him and put him on a drip, while Loveness sat helplessly by his side, fearing the worst. But Solomon was a fighter and he recovered and once again she took him home. Not two days later the thrush recurred, and he developed sores in his mouth. Loveness despaired but the HIV test on the baby had been negative, so why was he so sick?

For another three weeks, she and the baby spent more and more time at the hospital and once again, he was admitted. Roderick had grown more and more distant throughout the child's illness and Loveness learned that he had been living with yet another girl while she had been away. This was another girl about her own age, fresh from Bulawayo, and she suspected that he was still seeing her. Apart from her own pain at being betrayed, she wondered if this girl too was an innocent who would be infected by Roderick, and somewhere at the back of her mind was the thought that at least if she stayed with him, perhaps it would prevent him from infecting some other girl.

Loveness sat by the baby's cot in the hospital and watched anxiously as the nurse checked his breathing and his pulse. The diarrhoea had recurred, and she wondered helplessly how so much could come out of such a small body. He was listless and exhausted, his eyes dull and lifeless. She watched the nurse put the child down on the bed, and it was several minutes before she understood that he was dead. As she watched, life had fled from this, the seed of what was between her and Roderick. She thought of how her son had been, before he got sick, and how much he had suffered. And now his life was gone before he had even had a chance.

She couldn't touch the cold little body. She couldn't speak, or even cry. She just sat there, staring at him, until someone came and took the body away. Someone must have called Roderick, for all at once he was in the room, and Loveness stirred from her despair and stood up.

'Oh Roderick! The baby died, Roderick. I'm so sorry, the

baby died,' and she ran towards him and put her arms around him.

Roderick held her for a few minutes, and then he turned to his sister who had come with him, 'Take her. I want to see the baby,' and he went to the mortuary.

It was then that Roderick finally understood the reality of the infection he carried. It had come from him. Loveness had got it from him, and now it had claimed his child. His only son. All he had wanted was a son and of all the women he had had in his life none of them, except Loveness, had been able to give him that. But now his son was dead. It was one of the bitterest moments in Roderick's largely unrepentant life. His son was dead, and if his son was dead, then he too was dying. Never mind the outwardly healthy appearance. He too was going to die.

Together they left the hospital and that night he and Loveness sought the only comfort they knew. Loveness didn't even think about condoms, not until later, when the hospital finally confirmed that their baby had died of AIDS.

As was the custom, friends and relatives donated money to the family, *chema* to assist with the expenses of burial and looking after those who came to the funeral to pay their respects. Although many people gave them money, only a few came to the house to offer their condolences for they were all too aware of what had caused the baby's death. For Loveness, the whole period passed in front of her like something that was happening to someone else. She was aware that Roderick had quickly recovered from his grief over the loss of his only son. One evening she overheard Roderick's sisters arguing about money, and in the same breath heard them mention her baby. It was only then that she realised they were arguing how to split up their profits from the *chema*. She knew Roderick's sisters better now. Knew enough about them to appreciate that money was their primary preoccupation in life. Nothing else really seemed to matter to them.

Two of his sisters lived at home with their mother. The eldest was divorced. She had had three children and her husband had left the children with her until each reached the age of seven. Then he had called for them, and she had lost all contact with them. This, and the fact that he had never supported them while she cared for them had made her very bitter. No man wanted her while she had another man's children to bring up and once the children were grown, she was too old to attract another man. She spent her days imagining new ways to make money, even though she had a reasonably good job. Money was the only thing she seemed to care about. The other sister had never married. She was a coarse, loud woman who held her own with the men in the beerhalls and liked plenty of money to spend there. The only person she seemed to care about was her mother, of whom she was fiercely protective.

Roused from her grief, Loveness suddenly wondered if they had contacted her family to tell them about her child's death as they had claimed. She had – unreasonably – been upset that no representative of her family had put an appearance at the funeral. She went into the room to ask them about it and about her portion of the *chema*.

'What sort of people do you think we are?' Lydia, the oldest, responded angrily. 'Of course we told your family. We sent someone there, but your father only said it couldn't be his daughter we were talking about. He says he has no child called Loveness – that he only has two children.'

Could she believe her? But she really had no alternatives left to her.

'And as for the money, here, take this. Go and buy yourself a black dress so that you can show the world you are in decent mourning for your son.' She held out forty dollars. 'We didn't collect very much. I will give you seventy dollars later when we have counted out how much we spent on the funeral.' This was said in a dismissive tone and Loveness, already regretting her impulse to challenge them, turned away, the forty dollars for the dress in her hand. It was all she could do now for little Solomon, to show the world that she grieved for his loss. She didn't care about the money anyway, especially not if it might make her seem like them.

Chapter Seven

The next day when she was alone in the house, Loveness sat thinking back on her life and how miserable she was. Roderick was drinking a lot and when he came home drunk he insisted that they have sex. If she tried to resist he would beat her and all the time she was afraid that she would get pregnant again. Roderick seemed to dislike the pill as much as he disliked condoms and when he had found a packet in her bag he had made her tell him where the rest were and flushed them all down the toilet. She couldn't bear the thought that she might give birth to another child to suffer as little Solomon had. She could see only one way out of her misery. She decided to kill herself. She went to the kitchen and found a bottle of bleach. She took it to her room and was staring at it, wondering about the best way to drink it. Her whole mind was concentrated on the idea of escaping her life and she could hear nothing, not the sounds of the cars in the street outside, nor the children playing, not even the sound of Roderick's sister returning from her shopping.

The bedroom door opened just as she raised the bottle to her lips. Lydia rushed across the room and grabbed the bottle from her.

'What do you think you're doing you foolish child? Don't you know that it's a sin to take your own life!' and she left the room. Loveness lay down on the bed and wept. She couldn't even kill herself.

A few days later she was lifted enough from her despair to go and see Sister Gabriella. She told her nothing about the incident with the bleach but the nun seemed to know what was in her mind, and took her aside.

'Loveness, I've been wanting to talk to you for some time about the role God plays in all our lives. I want you to take this home with you and read this chapter,' and she took a large well-worn Bible from her bag. A chapter was marked, and Loveness took the book from her and read. It told how God had created man in his own image, and that only He who had given life had the right to take it away.

Loveness read on, and when the nun had finished her work and was ready to leave she said, 'I have had that Bible for many years. It was given to me when I was still a novice. I want you to have it now.'

'But I couldn't take it sister,' protested Loveness.

'Yes, you can. God wants you to hear his words. Take it, and read it. And remember. Anytime you want someone to talk to, I am here.'

For a while things between her and Roderick were slightly better and they decided to go back to Doctor Baker's. Roderick's sisters clearly didn't like having Loveness around and Roderick was all she had left now. She devoted herself to him completely for she knew no other way. When she had given herself to him it had been a statement of intention: she would spend the rest of her life with him and the love she had grown for him still burned strong, unhindered by the daily cruelties and the many dismissals he dealt her. It was surprising how easily she could deny the feelings of anger and betrayal which occasionally came to her in the middle of the night, or at odd times during the day.

At such times Loveness would read her Bible and slowly she determined that she would never try to take her own life again. She decided that what had happened to her was God's will and she must understand what it was He wanted her to do. If He wanted her to die from AIDS then that was what would happen, but in the meantime she must try to make sense of what was happening to her. What troubled her was Roderick's attitude towards her. Sometimes she even wondered if he hated her.

Despite the fact that he always spoke in favour of the use of condoms, Roderick refused absolutely to use them and in such a manner that she feared he would be violent if she persisted. With foreboding she noticed a tenderness in her breasts and was filled with a depression that seemed to block out all reasonable thought.

She went back for another pregnancy test and another HIV test. It was no surprise that both of them were positive. When she told Roderick the news – not about the HIV test, but about the pregnancy, he said nothing at first and then, 'Well, that's it then. We'll have to move out of here. Doctor Baker won't believe this one's because of condoms bursting too,' and two weeks later they were on their way to a small farm where the nuns had arranged for some land to be set aside for those suffering from AIDS and HIV.

The first few weeks there were almost happy. She and Roderick built their own small house and with no other disturbances, Loveness could almost convince herself that Roderick actually cared for her. She began to plough the small field that had been set aside for them. Their income was greatly reduced now that Roderick was less in touch with Doctor Baker and they would have to try and feed themselves.

Loveness was determined to do as much for herself as possible. Almost at the same pace as Loveness's determination grew, Roderick returned to his old habits and began to spend more and more time hanging around the bottle store.

Then one day she felt a stabbing pain in her abdomen, so sharp that she bent over and for a few seconds she could not breathe. Then it passed, and she continued to work but by evening she began to have cramping pains in her stomach. They felt like her labour pains with Solomon, but the pregnancy was not even five months yet.

The next day she went to the local clinic, and the nurses immediately sent word for Roderick that he must come and take her to the hospital. All the way on the bus he complained about the expense, asking her why she couldn't have come by herself. He left her at the hospital gates saying he would see her later, he wanted to visit his family.

The nurses in the hospital were cross with her and lectured her about risking her life by becoming pregnant again. Didn't she know that it was dangerous for her in her condition? Loveness just listened to them wearily. They removed the child, or what was left of it, the next day, but Loveness was very anaemic, and they insisted that she stay in hospital for another few days.

Finally they were willing to discharge her, not without several lectures about the use of condoms, or preferably abstaining from sex altogether. When she explained that Roderick would not allow her to use condoms, the nursestried to give her pills to take, so that at least she would not get pregnant again. But Loveness knew that Roderick would find them and take them away from her. After a quick conference one of the nurses asked her if she would like to have an injection that would stop her getting pregnant for three months at a time and she willingly agreed.

This worked for over a year. She managed to find excuses to come to town and have her injection and if Roderick wondered why she had not become pregnant again, he said nothing.

Isolated as they were on the farm, Loveness had a lot more time to think about what was happening to her, and about Roderick. She still grieved over little Solomon and each time she went to Harare, she would spend time with Sister Gabriella, talking about her child and her feelings about herself and what had happened to her. The nun had in some ways become a substitute mother to her.

Under the general stress and uncertainty of her life, Loveness's health began to deteriorate. She felt unwell a lot of the time, had a perpetual cough and never seemed to have any energy. Then she developed a particularly severe bout of diarrhoea and felt so bad that she almost asked Roderick to call Sister Gabriella. He was still rudely healthy although he was occasionally troubled by rashes, and the odd fever in the night. Most of his time was spent hanging around the nearby bottle store, and he rarely did anything to help. Even when she was really ill, Loveness would still drag herself up to make his food though she ate next to nothing herself. Fortunately, an AIDS counsellor who had the farm on his list happened to call by one day and left her with some drugs for her diarrhoea and some iron tablets and to her own surprise, within a few days, she was feeling quite well again. Roderick and she continued to have sex. It was not that Loveness felt any particular need to have sex, or even that she enjoyed it, but she knew that if he didn't have sex with her he would have it elsewhere, and out of her own misery and suffering the only light she could see was that she could prevent others from suffering as she had.

Loveness had never told Sister Gabriella or indeed anyone,

the truth about her relationship with Roderick and that she had been a virgin when they met. It was a matter of pride to her that she still loved him as much as she had that day so long ago when she had gone with him to Doctor Baker's. 'Love is good and kind, not selfish, seeking for itself,' she would say softly to herself, as if explaining to herself why she loved Roderick. It was to take considerably longer before Loveness arrived at the point of questioning Roderick's treatment of her and whether that also constituted love.

A few weeks after she had recovered from her bout of diarrhoea, she was carrying some water from the nearby well, and as she swung the container up onto her head her arm brushed hard against her breasts and she felt them hard and painful.

'Oh God,' she sent up a small prayer, 'I'm pregnant again. Oh please let me not be pregnant again.' She thought back. When had she had her last injection? That was it. She should have gone for another that time when she was sick, and she had been so sick she had forgotten all about it.

'Fool!' she chastised herself, for she knew it was impossible for her to have a child now; she couldn't face another failed pregnancy; another little Solomon.

She spent the next few days in fear and dread, hoping that she was wrong, wondering what bargain she could make with God to get rid of this life inside her, and then, quite early one morning, her back began to ache, and shortly she felt a wetness between her legs. When she found that it was blood, she was light-headed with relief. God had heard her prayers. It would be all right.

She spoke to one of the old women in the neighbouring village who told her to take it easy and lie down for a while. It was like this that Roderick found her when he returned from the bottle store looking for his supper.

'I'm sick, Roderick,' she replied.

'I'm bleeding,' she said. 'The old woman in the village says I should rest.'

'So what's new about that. It happens every month...' he began to say, but realised as he spoke that in fact it hadn't happened for a very long time now. He had supposed it was because she was anaemic.

'Are you pregnant again?' he asked her.

'I don't think this baby will live,' she answered. She had been bleeding quite heavily all day, whether she lay down or stood up seemed to make no difference, but she had no further pain.

'I think maybe I need to go to the clinic,' she said, without expecting him to agree.

'We have no money to waste on clinics,' he said, though they had plenty of money for him to buy beer. 'It will come out on its own,' and he left the hut.

Loveness watched the door close behind him, blocking out the rays of the setting sun and leaving her lost in the darkest shadow. She thought about herself, her life, and about God. She wondered if God really meant her to suffer like this. Was he the sort of God who enjoyed his people's suffering? Was he laughing now to see her like this? She found no answers. She drifted into sleep, and woke to feel Roderick climbing into the bed beside her. She got up to go to the toilet and found that the cloth she had used was soaked in blood. With some difficulty she groped around in the dark for another thicker cloth and returned to bed. Next morning she awoke feeling too lethargic to do anything for herself. The old woman from the village came to see her and brought her some porridge. Looking at the cloths Loveness discarded she said, 'Ah, ah, it's too much. You must go to the clinic my child. You are bleeding too much. Do you have pain?' and Loveness shook her head heavily, for she could feel nothing, nothing at all. The old lady held her head up and helped her eat the porridge, and drink some water. 'Where's your husband? He should take you to the clinic.'

Loveness shook her head again. 'We have no money for the clinic.'

'No money for the clinic? They'll look after you anyway in the state you're in. Tell me where your husband is and I'll fetch him. Is he in the field?'

Again Loveness shook her head. 'I suppose he's at the bottle store.'

'Tsk tsk tsk,' the old woman complained, and went about the room muttering to herself as she fetched a fresh cloth and removed the old ones.

'I'm leaving some water here,' she said, 'and later I'll bring you more porridge, but now I'm going to look for your husband.'

He wasn't difficult to find. He was, as always, at the centre of a laughing group of men. Their laughter stopped as the old woman approached, and she beckoned to Roderick to come to her so that she could speak to him.

'What do you want, old woman?' he said, 'Why are you bothering me?'

'I have come because your wife is sick. You must take her to the clinic.'

'She does not need to go to the clinic,' he said. 'The baby will come out on its own.'

'No, no. You are wrong. She is very sick. She is bleeding too much. You must take care of her. Why have you left her alone? You are her husband. You must take care of her.'

'I'm not her husband, you old witch. She dumped herself on me, and I don't have to do anything. It's her own fault she's in the state she's in,' and he brushed her aside and went back to the laughing crowd.

The old woman stood a while wondering what to do, and then made her way slowly home.

When she went back that evening to see Loveness she found her much as she had left her in the morning, but weaker. The bleeding seemed to have slowed down, but she could barely speak. Troubled, the old lady made her eat what she could, and was changing her cloth again when Roderick returned.

'What are you doing here, you witch?' He shouted at her. 'Don't you know this is my house? Get out. I don't want to see you here again.' He took hold of her bony old arm and threw her bodily out of the hut.

'You must care for her,' the old lady screamed at him, 'or you will have her death on your conscience.'

'Get on your way,' Roderick yelled after her, and closed the door.

He spoke to Loveness, but she must have been asleep because she did not reply. He made himself some supper, and went to bed.

Next day, he stayed by the hut. He didn't want that old witch interfering in his affairs. If she came back he would give her short shrift. Then he heard moaning from inside the hut, and went inside. Loveness was writhing in delirium on the bed, the cloth slipped from between her legs, and the congealed blood on it was beginning to smell. He realised that the room was thick with flies and now they all seemed to swarm towards the cloth. It was their infernal buzzing that had woken Loveness from her torpor. He raised her head and gave her some water to drink, and then he went out of the house to sit under the tree and drink the seven days' beer he had bought on his way home the night before.

All day Loveness lay half-conscious in the dark of the hut, her only company the flies that fed on her blood.

By evening of the next day, Roderick was getting bored. He was just deciding to go back to the bottle store when he heard the bus arriving. It pulled up at the bottle store and a few minutes later he was surprised to see two familiar figures coming towards him. It was his sister and his mother. He walked to meet them.

'What brings you here?'

'But didn't you send for us? We got a message that we must come because Loveness was very sick.'

'A message?' he said, half to himself, 'It must have been that nosey old witch from the village. She's not sick. She's having another miscarriage. I don't know why she keeps getting pregnant. You'd think she'd have more sense after the baby died.'

His mother ignored him, and went towards the hut. When she opened the door she gasped and turned her head away from the stench that greeted her. Holding her breath she tried again and this time prepared, she entered the hut.

Loveness lay semi-conscious, much as Roderick had left her that morning. She called her daughter.

'Come here, we must get her out of here. There's blood and flies everywhere.'

For once she was angry with her son.

'How could you leave her like this? She's very sick. Why didn't you take her to the clinic before she got so bad? Do you want her to die?'

'She's going to die anyway.' Roderick replied sulkily. 'What difference does it make whether it's now or later.'

His mother just looked at him, and continued to clean up Loveness.

'I think we'll have to take her to Harare on the bus. They can't do anything for her at the clinic when she is in this state. She must have lost a lot of blood.' She held water to Loveness's lips, and the girl roused herself enough to open her eyes.

'Loveness. We have to take you to Harare on the bus. Can you understand me?'

She was answered by a faint nod of the head.

'Okay. Roderick, run and tell the driver to wait for us. Now, I'm going to put some clean clothes on you. Then you must help us to take you to the bus.'

Loveness moaned in reply.

Somehow they got to the bus and from there to the hospital. No questions were asked. They simply rushed her to the theatre, where they gave her another D and C and then moved her back to the ward, where they gave her several units of blood.

As Loveness slowly recovered, she understood how close she had come to having no more future, even if what was left to her now was very short. She remembered the kindness of the old lady who had tried to care for her at the village and with horror, she remembered Roderick chasing her saviour away, sitting like a vulture outside the hut while the flies buzzed mercilessly around her. What could she do? The words she had read in the Bible came to her again, 'Love is…'. The only love she had ever really known was her father's and she saw his face as she had last seen him – resigned, hurt and disappointed.

She must have fallen asleep and she awoke full of a sense of longing to correct the wrongs she had done to her father. She opened her eyes to see Sister Gabriella sitting by her side.

Sister Gabriella reached out and stroked her forehead.

'How are you feeling, my dear?'

'Sister Gabriella!' Tears rushed into her eyes as she recognised the one person in all the world she could trust.

'Oh, how good of you to come. I've been so alone ...' and she began to sob.

Sister Gabriella let her cry, and then she said softly, 'And what are you going to do now, Loveness? The nurses told me what happened. How did you get into such a state?'

Loveness looked into the nun's eyes and she knew she couldn't protect Roderick anymore. Lying in the hut, she had felt his hatred coming at her through the walls. She realised now how misplaced her love for him had been. Roderick could not love anyone except himself, and perhaps not even that.

'It was Roderick, sister. He wouldn't take me to the clinic. He said we didn't have money, and then an old lady tried to help me and he chased her away. He stayed by the hut all day and he did nothing for me, only gave me some water in the morning. If the old woman hadn't called his mother I think I would have died there. And the flies, oh the flies...' tears came again as the nightmare came back to her. 'I can't go back to him, sister, I can't.'

Her voice was raised in a question as though she thought the nun might force her to stay with the monster she had loved.

'There there, dear. Don't upset yourself. In fact, I was hoping you'd come and stay with us for a while, until you're feeling better and have decided what you want to do.'

Loveness's whole being flooded with relief and for the first time since Solomon had died, she felt the stirrings of hope in her heart.

Chapter Eight

For a few weeks Loveness stayed with Sister Gabriella and recuperated, but the cough she had for several months refused to go away and eventually she went to the doctor. After some exploratory tests, he told her that she had TB and would have to be admitted into the hospital for infectious diseases.

During her stay with Sister Gabriella, the two often talked about Loveness's childhood, and her family, but Loveness never dared tell her friend how she had come to living in Mufakose and how she had met Roderick. She feared that Sister Gabriella would reject her, such a cruel and selfish daughter, but through their talks, Loveness came to understand herself better and to see that it was her own choices that had brought her here.

The diagnosis of TB was another crisis in her young life. She had heard about TB and HIV and she feared that it meant she was dying, that now she had AIDS. She began to appreciate how destructive her relationship with Roderick had been – that it was based on dependence more than on love. She saw too that he had never loved her and in time she even pitied him. She thought more about her own family and saw how wrong she had been, all the mistakes she had made through being selfish, in not thinking about her own future. She determined that if she got well again she would do everything in her power to make up for her mistakes. She also felt more strongly than ever the need to see her father again.

One day, when Sister Gabriella came to see her she said, 'Sister. Could you do me a favour?' Sister Gabriella looked at her with kindly surprise, for Loveness had rarely asked for anything.

'Of course, my dear. What is it?'

'It's my father.' Loveness looked down at her hands lying on the pink hospital blanket and took a deep breath.

'I know I treated my family, but especially him, very badly. I ran away, you know. I lied to him, and I even stole his money. I never told you this before. That was before I met Roderick. Then when I got pregnant I wanted to get away from Roderick because, by then, you see, I knew that I was infected, and I had nowhere else to go, so I went home, but my father wouldn't even talk to me. He wasn't cruel,' she added quickly, in case the nun should get the wrong impression of her father, 'but he just didn't want anything to do with me. And I can understand why. But now. Well, I think I understand life a little better. If it weren't for that old woman I might have died. But I'm alive and I would like to make amends to my father, to be with my family again. But you see, here I am in trouble again and looking for him. I would understand if he didn't want me back.' She looked up at her friend. 'I thought perhaps if you got in touch with him and explained then maybe he would agree to see me?'

'Of course, child. In fact, I'll go and speak to him myself, as soon as I can get permission from the mother superior.' For the remainder of the visiting hour, they talked about Loveness's family, and how everything had started to go wrong.

One afternoon, Loveness sat in a chair on the verandah outside her ward, thinking how beautiful everything looked in the sunshine and realised that she actually felt better than she had in a long time.

It was as she was pondering this new feeling that she heard a man's voice behind her saying hesitantly, 'Loveness?'

Her heart leapt at the sound of that well-loved voice.

'Father!' she cried, jumping out of her chair and running towards him. She threw her arms about him and as he gently rocked her in his arms she murmured against his shoulder, 'Oh father, thank you, thank you. Thank you for coming. I can't believe you came. I never thought you would...' Over his shoulder, she saw Sister Gabriella quietly withdraw.

After their initial greeting they were a little strange with each other, these two people who were so important to one another. Solomon had found it hard to ignore her appeal for help that dreadful time over a year ago and had often wanted to try and find his daughter, but he was also afraid, for he had never been able to understand how Loveness had turned out as she had. Perhaps she would never change. When Sister Gabriella came to see him, and told him about the Loveness she knew, and that she was in hospital with TB, he had felt his hard heart soften and before she could actually make her request that he agree to see her, he interrupted her.

'Sister, when you return to Harare, I will go with you to see my daughter.' The nun's face lit up in reply and together they had driven to Harare.

At last, Loveness began to tell her father what had happened to her, about the death of her child and finally, about her HIV infection. This last was very difficult. As she spoke, she watched her father's face fall in defeat – had he found her again only to have her taken away by death? She vowed that she would live long enough to make up to him some of the sorrow she had caused. How could she die now and hurt her beloved father again?

To her surprise and absolute joy, when she had been in the hospital for three weeks, the doctor came to her and told her she was releasing her. She was no longer infectious and had responded so well to the medication that she should make a full recovery. She heard the surprise in the doctor's voice as she told her the news even though she tried to conceal it, for Loveness had been very weak when she arrived and the doctor had seen many cases like hers. Usually they failed to respond to treatment and after a few weeks they died.

Loveness had no doubt that this unexpected reprieve was a gift from God and she immediately set about her promised task. She returned to her family in Redcliff and recuperated, restoring her relationship with her father, delighting in the new found trust and sharing between them. Meantime, she was making plans. When she was decreed fit enough to work, she moved back to Harare and attended counselling training sessions, learning everything she could about AIDS and HIV. Soon she was counselling others in her situation and each weekend she went home to Redcliff and spent time with her family. She was so busy that she forgot about her own ailments, and it was only after a few months of her new-found occupation when Sister Gabriella came to visit her, that she realised how well she was feeling.

'You've gained weight, Loveness!' said the nun.

Nonplussed, Loveness looked at herself and saw that it was true.

'Oh, sister!' she cried. 'I never knew I could do anything like this! I feel so much better about myself, about Roderick, about everything. Thank you so much for seeing my father and bringing him to see me. Now I really feel I can do some good, and I even enjoy it and guess what, they've offered me a job in the Bulawayo branch of AWC.'

'That's wonderful news, my dear,' said the sister, smiling warmly at her protégé. 'I knew things would work out for the best. Are you going to take it?'

Loveness looked at her in surprise. 'But of course I'm going to take it. This is my life now. And however short or long it may be, I'm going to do what I can with it. I wasted so much of my life and I know I don't have much time left. I've got to do as much as I can.'

Sister Gabriella couldn't reply. The self-assured young woman standing before her was like another person. She thought back to how she had been when she visited her in the hospital, and looked again at Loveness. Surely this was one of God's miracles?

After Loveness's departure for Bulawayo, Sister Gabriella saw less of her, but she often heard about her from other people, and occasional letters passed between them. Roderick had ceased to come to the nuns' afternoon sessions in the church hall.

Doctor Baker was the only one in whom Loveness confided the whole story of her relationship with Roderick, including the fact that he was responsible for her infection. The doctor was extremely angry and had made a half-hearted attempt to get Loveness to sue Roddy, but in her new-found happiness and self-possession, Loveness had no room to hate Roderick. Instead she pitied him. She had heard that he had started to develop the symptoms of full-blown AIDS and she, more than anyone, knew how lonely and afraid he must feel. She knew how frightened he would be in the long lonely nights, and now that it was obvious he had AIDS he would not be able to fool any other young girl into taking him on. Perhaps he might find another HIV girl to stay with him, but he would have to learn to treat her better than was his way. Sometimes her heart would fill with pain for him. She had loved him so much and he hadn't even been capable of seeing that love and accepting it for what it was.

With Loveness's departure, Roderick seemed to have lost some of his confidence. He was haunted by the idea that she might tell others the truth, and was convinced that everyone knew about him. Doctor Baker had told him in no uncertain terms what he thought of him and told him he was lucky that Loveness was such a good person. He stopped going to the AWC, frightened that the doctor would tell them the truth. He couldn't believe that Loveness would not take the opportunity to tell everyone how he had treated her and eventually he returned to his mother's home, and lived almost as a recluse on the money he claimed from the social welfare people and the agency he had once done some work for.

As Loveness became more and more involved in the struggle against AIDS, Roderick's grew weaker and became more and more debilitated until the inevitable happened. He developed pneumonia, and in a few days he was dead. Sister Gabriella went to the hospital to see him, but he was too weak to know she was there. After his death, she called Loveness to tell her what had happened and she insisted on coming to the funeral. True to form, his sisters were reluctant to remove the body from the mortuary and it was Loveness who organised the coffin, and Loveness who stood beside the grave when all the others had long departed.

Sister Gabriella approached her and said, 'You've done all you can, my child. Come now and we'll go home.'

Stirred from her reverie, Loveness looked up at her.

'You know sister, if you see a lion in the path you run away.

Roderick was a lion out to kill me, but I didn't realise it and I offered myself to him. It wasn't all his fault. But now the lion is dead, and I'm still here.' There was a hint of wonder in her voice.

Not long after, Sister Gabriella was reading the newspaper, when she came across an article headed, 'HIV positive girl to attend International AIDS Conference in Brussels.' She looked at the photograph of a shyly smiling Loveness waiting to board a plane, and marvelled at the wondrous things that God had done.

That was a year ago and despite all the predictions to the contrary, Loveness is still going strong. She has a new lease on life, and lives each day as it comes, as positively and effectively as she can, and her father is proud to say, 'Oh yes. That's my daughter, Loveness.'

Some useful explanations

Below is an explanation of some useful terms in the era we are in today, when HIV can be prevented and treated.

AIDS is short for Acquired immune deficiency syndrome, in which the body's immune system (the defence against disease) is weakened lowering a person's resistance to infection and malignancy. It is a result of untreated HIV infection. It is caused by a virus (the human immunodeficiency virus, or HIV), which is transmitted through body fluids during unprotected sex and through blood-to-blood transmission, as well as from an infected mother to her baby during pregnancy, delivery and breastfeeding. HIV is a manageable chronic condition, provided medication is taken as prescribed.

Antiretroviral medicine (ARV) ARV medicines help people living with HIV live long and healthy lives. Usually a person takes a combination of three different ARVs, often combined in a single pill. They must be taken exactly as instructed!

CD4 count. This is a laboratory test to see how many CD4 cells are in a person's blood sample. The average person has a CD4 count of between 500 and 1500. When you are HIV positive, the virus attacks the CD4 cells and the CD4 count gradually drops as the infection progresses. The CD4 count shows how well the immune system is working and also shows how well ARV treatment is working

Condom. This is used during sexual intercourse (male condoms are worn on a man's penis and female condoms inside a woman's vagina) as a barrier to reduce the risk of HIV and sexually transmitted infections (STIs) Used correctly condoms also prevent pregnancy.

Discrimination. This is the unjust treatment of someone because of race, age, sex, gender, or HIV positive status, among others.

HIV. Stands for human immunodeficiency virus – the virus that, left untreated, leads to AIDS. There is no cure for HIV, but it can be managed, just like other chronic, life long medical conditions like diabetes and high blood pressure, by taking regular medication – in this case, ARVs.

HIV prevention. This means the various ways of preventing HIV transmission, e.g. abstinence (not having sex at all), condom use, PEP (post-exposure prophylaxis), PREP (pre-exposure prophylaxis), prevention of mother-to-child transmission (PMTCT), voluntary medical male circumcision (VMMC) and taking ARVs.

Medical male circumcision. This is the surgical removal of the foreskin of the penis by a trained healthcare provider. It lowers the risk of HIV infection in men. Circumcised men should still use condoms.

Post-exposure prophylaxis (PEP) is a short course of ARVs taken after possible exposure to HIV, e.g. through rape or after a condom burst. PEP must be taken within 72 hours of the event and can be obtained from any PSI facility, or through a doctor or clinic.

PMTCT. Prevention of mother-to-child transmission (PMTCT) means services to prevent an HIV-positive mother passing HIV to her baby during pregnancy, labour, delivery, or breastfeeding.

Stigma. This is someone, for example, an HIV positive person, is disapproved of by people because of it. Stigma goes often hand-in-hand with shame. It can result in threats and abuse and generally leads to discrimination.

Transactional sex. This is when sex is exchanged for other benefits like food, housing, transport money, school fees and other items.

Undetectable viral load (see also CD4 count). Viral load is a laboratory test to check how much HIV is in 1ml of someone's blood. If the viral load is below 10,000 their HIV is under control, but the aim is to be undetectable – in other words, the machine cannot find it. When a person's viral load is undetectable they are very unlikely to infect another person, but they are still HIV positive and need to continue taking their ARVs as instructed.

CPSIA information can be obtained
at www.ICGtesting.com
Printed in the USA
LVHW050613291222
736079LV00005B/591

9 781779 223319